SHOWDOWN AT THE KODIAK STARPORT

Other Titles by Justin Oldham

Bibix
Tales from the Kodiak Starport
Crisis at the Kodiak Starport

SHOWDOWN AT THE KODIAK STARPORT

BY JUSTIN OLDHAM

SHADOW FUSION LLC
ANCHORAGE

Published in the United States of America by Shadow Fusion LLC
http://www.shadowfusionbooks.com

Cover images courtesy of NASA/JPL-Caltech and NASA Visible Earth (visibleearth.nasa.gov)

Translations from English to Mandarin Chinese courtesy of Google Translate

Library of Congress Control Number: 2015919993

ISBN: 978-1-935964-70-4

This book is dedicated to the pioneering spirit of Alaskans everywhere, in all times and places. The conspirators who made this incarnation of the Kodiak Starport a reality are appreciated. You know who you are.

PROLOGUE

The starport has become more than a place where rockets and spaceships launch and land. It's a cross-genre literary construct that writers have used as a backdrop for all sorts of intrigues, ranging from action to romance. As a real world institution that supports interplanetary space travel, the starport became everything science fiction writers dreamed it could be—and much more.

Corporate power makes the starport a formidable force on any world or inhabited body that has one. Rivalries between competing terrestrial facilities resulted in the period's most notable aerospace technical achievements. Friction between sovereign governments and commercial starports sparked a new space race that redefined Asia-Pacific diplomacy for the remainder of the 21st Century.

As popular as they were, no sovereign government of that era could match or exceed the economic potential of multi-national commercial conglomerates. Taxes and tariffs meant to curb the behaviors of big business were a mere hindrance to multinationals because their interests weren't constrained by geographic borders. High fees and extreme penalties in some countries would be offset by lower operating costs in others. Cooperative nations got more consideration from interested firms that wanted to establish new factories, distribution centers, or training facilities.

The effects of pollution and a changing global climate are widely regarded as important socio-political factors in this period. The Chinese-American conflict that altered the balance of power throughout the Asia-Pacific region was typical of the resource wars that left their marks before the 21st Century ended. Each fight for food and water was motivated by fears of starvation, though greed, secular politics, and religion added to the intensity of each conflict.

Was the decline of national power inevitable? Circumstances that led to the collapse of many governments couldn't always be anticipated. Contemporary thinkers believe these outcomes were avoidable. If 20th Century civic leaders had been able to work with each other in spite of such obvious differences, it's possible that globe-spanning commercial concerns might have learned to function with a similar conscience.

Experts are in general agreement that the Kodiak starport and its parent company are typical for their day. Geopolitics, as they affected these entities, are still being studied in an effort to understand the breakdown of national power that occurred during this war. The Small Rock Mine disaster and its effect on Bristol Bay appear to be just one of many environmental nightmares that unfolded in the background, though it seems to have had a greater impact on starport operations than some historians are willing to concede.

Allegations in the media and formal complaints through agencies and embassies filed against starport administrators and senior staff suggested that there was some wrong-doing on their parts during and after the Asia-Pacific campaign. Present-day researchers are still struggling to examine some of the more controversial decisions that were made by corporate staff and contractors during those pivotal moments. These investigations continue to be hampered by the untimely loss of original documents.

What you're about to read is a dramatic recreation of significant events, based on conjecture, third party recollections, official sources, media reportage, and viewpoints extrapolated from published memoirs.

Chapter One

Two years after the war started, conditions throughout the Asia-Pacific region were dire as warships and submarines from a dozen nations prowled the China Seas and Pacific Ocean in search of targets that were getting harder to find. Loss of satellite reconnaissance and global positioning systems early in the conflict caused a sudden technological regression that reduced all navies to old-fashioned shoot-on-sight tactics that few crews had firsthand experience with.

Armed vessels equipped with anti-submarine helicopters, multirole VTOLs, and jump jets of all sorts became the most important assets in their respective fleets when observation from space was no longer an option. High-tech fire control systems were suddenly limited to what local radars could detect. Remotely-piloted drones were more valuable than they had been, though their controllable range was greatly reduced.

Famines on land combined with the loss of food from the sea to drive the politics that made this war possible as droughts continued. Kodiak Starport's *Gold Rush* space station was destroyed by a near miss from Chinese-launched nuclear ordnance. That event had been witnessed by millions of agitated viewers on live television as worldwide communications failed.

An even larger subscribership saw the destruction of a Chinese aircraft carrier. The infamous Sasha Xavier had unleashed an improvised one-shot rail gun, illegally concealed aboard *Gold Rush*, shortly before the descending platform's digital cameras failed. Though she was widely believed to be dead, rumors of an off-the-grid existence persisted. "Sasha sightings" continued to be reported by tabloids and bloggers two years after her disappearance.

The use of nuclear weapons wasn't limited to the destruction of orbital platforms. The balance of power was altered on terrestrial battlefields as the second miserable wartime winter engulfed a hungry world. Lesser nations, forced to defend scarce sources, resorted to defensive releases to create safe zones between themselves and larger adversaries.

The decision to neutralize Japan's vigorous Tokyo Starport in such a determined and permanent way was viewed by experts in Beijing as unavoidably necessary. Consensus among Central Committee leaders was reached after months of debate. They reasoned that long-term socioeconomic considerations outweighed environmental costs by the slimmest of margins.

"Us or them," an internal memorandum summarized. To avoid political repercussions, a theater-level plan was developed for the western naval zones that would be affected. It called for a series of broadly worded military and commercial conditions to be met. On-site authority would allow regional commanders with access to nuclear warheads to fire long range cruise missiles against the Tokyo starport, if they observed what was expected to be a rare opening in Japan's layered defenses.

Time passed. An attentive intelligence officer was promoted to command a subterranean launch site on the peninsula north of Qingdao. He realized that all conditions of the classified order had been met on a cold winter's night as everyone else in the region prepared to relax for the Christmas holiday. The attack order was given. Battery personnel acted promptly.

* * *

Damp December wind roared in off the Bering Sea to stir gritty snow in to a fine, gray haze. Visibility on

Kodiak Island decreased to a matter of yards within minutes as rain and hail covered roads and buildings with a coarse glaze that wouldn't melt for weeks.

Starport activity continued without any letup, in spite of the inconveniences posed by this seasonable variable that would've shut down most terrestrial airports. Streetlamps and structural perimeter lights were deliberately left on, in spite of wartime threats.

Local and regional air defense systems, once camouflaged and kept secret because their ownership had been somewhat questionable before the outbreak of hostilities, were now openly guarded by uniformed starport personnel who could be seen by anyone who passed near their fortified emplacements.

Snowplows, escorted by marked security vehicles, rumbled up and down icy roads to keep them clear for commercial and civil traffic. Many of these short processions were often trailed by long lines of delivery vans or four-wheel drive automobiles. Many of the people who worked in and around the starport thought of regular snow clearance and the obvious deployment of anti-missile systems as good signs for the future.

Air defense coordinator Norman Ahgupuk, wearing a flight suit festooned with starport logos and corporate markings, walked into in his office underneath the aviation annex. He stared at his name and job title on the door. The wet soles of his insulated boots squeaked on the new synthetic carpet.

A simulated window that looked so very real hung on the far wall. Its dynamic digital image showcased a winter skyline, as if he were viewing the scene from a high corner office. Digital readouts around the room proclaimed the local time to be 7:40 p.m.

"Outside camera," he reminded himself. "Nobody has a window. Not anymore."

Engineers worked round the clock to rebuild as much of the starport as they could during the warmer months.

Essential personnel and equipment were relocated to offices and worksites underground. Surface-level buildings appearing to have windows were actually fitted with solar collectors intended to simulate the appearance of habitation.

The retired U.S. Air Force officer stood in the open doorway to survey his assigned space. Everything in the room was new, except for dozens of mementos on the walls that attested to his former career as a military aviator. Those accessories included a helmet of an older style with his last squadron insignia and call sign emblazoned on it.

"Do you like this?" a facilities manager asked while approaching from behind. Full spectrum digital illumination filled the room with soft yellow light designed to mimic sunlight.

"Anyone else here?" Norman asked, just to change the subject.

"No, sir," the specialist nodded while pointing at his watch, "Everyone is gone for the holiday. Christmas is just two days away. I'm here because you're here. If you're satisfied with the arrangements, we can sign a few things and be on our way."

The aging pilot eyed the recently varnished birch desk that dominated the small room. "That's an old piece of furniture. Has it been restored?"

"Right," the detail-oriented man smiled. "Inventory said it was in your dad's office when he was here. We pulled it from storage and cleaned it up. Thought you might like a link to the past. Of course, we could—"

"Thanks," Norman grinned, "Go get your pad. Everything's fine just the way it is."

The attentive fellow took a step back. "That chair came with the desk, too."

Ahgupuk shuffled into the room while the manager went to get his handheld computer. Norman laid a hand on the restored wooden chair and studied its leather cushion, imagining his father working at that desk as head of security for the growing starport two decades earlier.

"Not exactly what you had in mind, is it?"

Norman pivoted to see an elderly man in a dark suit and tie wearing wire-rimmed glasses leaning on a cane in the doorway.

"Can I help you?" he asked.

"I know that look," the older gentleman confided with a nod of his bald head. "You're askin' yourself a lot of hard questions right now."

Norman paused to take a closer look at his unexpected interrogator. A badge clipped to his lapel indicated the man was a senior technology advisor. The large red letter "A" next to his photo indicated he had full access.

Ahgupuk squinted to make out the man's name. "Have we met?"

"Not formally," Ivan Gallagher admitted. "I've been through your hangars a few times. Nothing official. Just looking."

Norman rested both hands on the back of his chair. "Rumor has it that you're never here. Nothing official."

"I'm not here now," Ivan emphasized. "Neither are you. We're both at home having a nice holiday meal with family and friends."

Ahgupuk watched the view from his simulated window for several seconds as he weighed his options. "Okay. I'll bite. What's this all about?"

"Do you have any hobbies?" Gallagher wondered.

"I collect tribal art," Norman replied casually.

The electronics executive pointed with his cane. "You've also been looking around for any hint of military space planes."

"How's that a hobby?"

Ivan shook his hairless head. "You've been told to leave that alone. Got your own planes to fly, but no, you're still lookin' for something you shouldn't find."

"They *do* exist," Norman concluded. "I knew it! Why wasn't I—"

The old Alaskan let the tip of his cane fall to the floor with an audible click. "You and I have one thing in common. We're both too old. We couldn't make the leap to that sort of thing. Not even if we wanted to."

Norman was angry. He came around his chair in two strides. "All I wanted—"

"Hold your horses!" Ivan barked. "Look out the window. What do you see?"

"It's not a real window!"

"My company made it," Gallagher bragged. "I'll call it whatever I like. Now. Don't mess around. Tell me. What do you see?"

Norman looked over his shoulder. "Lights. Buildings. Night. Sky. What else am I looking for?"

Ivan took a few slow steps in to the room, stopping next to the taller man. "It works because we work. We do our jobs. One screw up, and it sets off a chain reaction that runs through the whole operation. Slow loading. Slow fueling. Sloppy turnaround. Anything can go wrong."

"If you can keep it well-defended."

"That's where you and I fit in," Ivan insisted. "We have our own jobs. You make sure those refurbished F-15s get pilots. I get you the best possible aviation electronics for those relics. We're doing this without bothering the nice men and women who couldn't possibly be doing what you think they might be."

"You don't fly," Norman huffed. "I wouldn't expect you to understand. It's the closest thing to space any of us are ever going to see. It's not stick and rudder. Nobody flies a military space plane. Most of it is done with computers. We could—"

"I see," Gallagher laughed. "You think you're being cheated. Is that it? You wanted a chance to fly in space and you feel locked out."

"Wouldn't you?"

Ivan shook his pale head. "I'd give a lot to put my company's avionics into whatever it is they're building. Some of the better people who used to work for me might be doing it right now. I don't know. As much as I want it, I'm not up to the challenge. Not anymore. So, I leave it to the people who are."

"Why can't we see it?"

The older man tapped his cane on floor. "What purpose would that serve? Tell me."

Agphupuk hesitated. "They should know."

"Why?"

Norman walked around his desk. "Secrecy does make for good security. I'll grant you that. Even if they aren't in on this, I want to be."

"That's the truth of it," Ivan confided. "*You'd* like to know. Don't think for a minute that I see this any differently than do you, just because I don't fly the planes. I've spent my whole life putting parts in them. I know where they can go and what they can do. That makes me curious. Just as nosy as you are right now."

The pilot was insulted. "We'd do our jobs better if we knew—"

"That's not your choice to make!" Gallagher scolded.

"Are you here to warn me off?"

Ivan looked over his shoulder. "No. Not at all. I don't mind it when the guys who run this place get some grief for keeping their secrets. Look." He fidgeted. "One troublemaker to another, I'd like to help you scratch that itch, if you'll keep quiet about what you see."

The combat veteran looked at the images being transmitted through his false window while gathering his thoughts. "We're protecting this place with a mixed bag of old birds flown by oddballs. They rely on air defense and missile systems that were obsolete before I was born. All of us could do our jobs better if we knew there was something a bit more substantial to back us up."

The businessman nodded. "C'mon, use your head. They're not telling us because we don't need to know. Nobody has denied anything, they're just not—"

"What are you getting at?"

"Wanna borrow my hearing aid?" Gallagher quipped. "You wanted to see military space planes. Let's go have a look, on the condition that you drop this whole thing and never say another word about it to anyone."

"You're breaking the rules?" Norman guessed.

"What they don't know won't hurt me."

The pilot sobered. "Been reading about the Chinese space planes for quite some time. Yes. I want to see the future. How many do we have?"

The older man shifted his stance. "We never had this conversation. And there are no such vehicles under development at this facility. You're at home this evening, with a full stomach, complaining about your job."

"Of course," Norman acknowledged.

"All right, then." Ivan perked up. "We own stock in this company. Let's go have a look at our space planes. I haven't seen 'em. If you say one word about this to anyone—"

"I get it," Ahgupuk interjected.

"Not even to your best pilots!"

Norman reached for his coat. "You can do this without repercussions?"

"Holiday fever," Ivan observed, "Everyone else with a brain is where you should be."

"That manager is coming back with—"

The engineer shuffled backward toward the door, "I sent him home. You can do all that paperwork later."

Norman shrugged in to his parka. "Can I see one of the cockpits?"

"No!" Gallagher admonished while retreating in to the hallway.

CHAPTER TWO

Moonlight cast a platinum glow over the snow-covered city as a droning VTOL settled on an ice-covered helipad at the University of Alaska's densely packed Anchorage campus. Navigation lights illuminated the bold blue Kodiak Starport logo on either side of the long, sleek, black airframe as the vehicle landed.

Vectored thrust allowed the aircraft to touch down loudly in a swirl of ice and snow inside a brightly lighted perimeter. Cargo doors opened with a clunk. Men and women in body armor and urban camouflage streamed out of the aircraft. Harsh perimeter lighting made them stand out against the night. Some of them ignored the cold to stand at distant points around the wide open area, gripping automatic weapons in thermal sleeves, while others went in through the nearest entrance.

The troopship lifted off with bay doors open seconds after the last guardian leapt out. Headset radios chattered as a dozen soldiers set up their safety zone.

"Exterior sentries in place."

"Interior checked and posted."

"Units on station. Administrator, land when ready."

Thirty seconds passed. None of the snow-covered veterans moved from where they stood as the wind blew. Some looked up at the sound of a fast-approaching aircraft. Battery powered thermal underwear kept them warm as a second ship, superficially identical to the one they'd arrive in, rushed up from a low altitude. It approached for a rapidly turning touchdown.

Cargo doors slid open to reveal a luxurious interior. Cabin lighting had been turned down before landing. Four people in bright yellow cold weather gear came out of a nearby shelter to place wheel chocks, which would prevent the tilt-rotor machine from shifting.

A pair of armed and armored starport guards were the first to step out, followed by a line of staffers in trendy clothes wrapped in equally expensive coats. They exited in a hurry while the aircrew tended to their duties.

Senior administrator James Cook stepped out of the advanced helicopter with a battered briefcase in one hand, wearing a blue parka littered with old and new starport logos. He was followed by a female guard with officer's rank in body armor with a pistol snug inside a shoulder holster. She carried an older encrypted communications device, disguised to look like an ordinary piece of aluminum luggage, in one gloved hand.

The open front of Cook's insulated jacket flapped in the fading breeze of the rotor wash as he made his way toward a glass and steel entryway.

"Still glad you took the job?" he asked her.

"Wouldn't miss this for the world," Kelly Haines replied, smiling and matching his stride. A headset radio chirped and crackled in her ears.

Jim raised his briefcase to shield his face from flying ice fragments as passengers found their way off the landing pad, into a warm lounge. "Go to work."

Haines gave orders to one of her subordinates. Cook went inside while she directed his protection detail for the first time in a public setting as the senior specialist. Her qualifications as an experienced team leader and communications liaison allowed him to travel light, with one less person aboard his transport.

That was more than a fuel saving measure. It meant one less job to fill in a professional climate where skilled workers in every field were hard to come by. Corporate headhunters now competed with governments and military recruiters for candidates at every wage and education level as mandatory military enlistments drained labor pools.

Jim followed the person ahead of him into the lounge. Carefully designed mood lighting was accentuated by dark wood and antique display cases that featured artifacts from Alaska's past behind double-paned glass, sealed within inert gases against destructive pollutants.

He found an empty chair near the silent bank of elevators and put his briefcase in it. A pair of campus security guards in formal dark blue dress uniforms met with members of his security team as the reception area filled with peripatetic people. Urban camouflage and body armor with compact automatic weapons contrasted sharply with the unarmed ceremonial duo that was there to work with them.

"Where's the campus president?" Jim asked the gray-haired man with lieutenant's stripes on his arm. "I wanted to have a few words with him before we got started."

"Scheduling conflict," Latham apologized.

"I'm having a day like that," the executive grumped while fingering his white hair back into place.

"No offense is intended," the officer insisted when he noticed Cook's displeasure. "We've all got the same problem. It's year two of the war. Selective Service has called up most of the people who can fight. That leaves us a bit shorthanded."

The starport boss looked around. He saw Haines working her way towards him as she conferred with civilian staff. "This is the season for giving," he fussed while peeling off his coat. "So, here I am with presents. What's your boss like? I've never met him. Chatted a few times through social media. What's he like?"

"Nice guy," the lieutenant decided while his aide coordinated with starport personnel to connect with local wireless networks. "This career day isn't going well."

"It's hard to be optimistic when everything you worked for is coming apart at the seams," Jim empathized after an orbiting guard took his coat. "You wouldn't believe... Never mind. I put a hole in my schedule every year to do this. Rain or shine. Peace or war. I know what kind of day he's having."

"Yes, sir," Latham nodded.

Jim eyed the dial on his stainless steel wristwatch. "Chancellor Hathaway wanted this shindig at UAA, so here I am. Let's give my team a few minutes."

"Nice timepiece," the officer appreciated, "Can't remember the last time I saw a chronograph like that."

Cook handled the folds and creases in his dark suit. "Every starport boss gets one," he recalled, "Legend says the guy who started this tradition sent his watch into space because he couldn't go."

"Has this been to space?"

"Twice," Jim acknowledged.

"Why didn't you go with it?"

Jim rubbed a finger around the face of his old fashioned timepiece. "Too much to do. Never enough time to be that selfish."

The uniformed representative surveyed his surroundings. "It takes a lot to run this campus. Keeping it secure is no picnic."

"Wanna trade jobs?" the exasperated executive quipped while knotting his dark silk neck tie.

The middle-aged man laughed. "I was a neighborhood cop for twenty years before taking this job. I'm in a good place. Know what I'm saying?"

Cook leaned over to tie his shoe lace. "A few wise words in young ears," he surmised. "Let 'em think the right thing to do was their idea."

"That's it, right there," the lieutenant affirmed. "My boss knows you're here. We'd give you the red carpet treatment, if we could, because you are a major sponsor about to hand over a big check. This is all we have, so this is what you get."

"Smart." Jim stood up and reached for a tablet computer that was given to him by a passing aide. "Fair enough. Its 8:05 p.m. Would you at least tell me if the festivities are still on track? Do I make my speech at 8:15, or what?"

Latham spoke briefly with his own subordinate. "We haven't heard anything to the contrary," he advised. "Let me show you the way. Over there, to the elevator."

"Let them go first," Jim suggested. "I'll stay here 'til the front end is on-site."

The officer didn't argue. He sent his partner ahead with two of the starport soldiers. "Are you expecting trouble, or have you had trouble?" he asked when the elevator doors closed.

"Both," Cook confided.

"Five minutes," an assistant whispered, "and look at your news."

Jim glanced at his tablet that was silently scrolling video. "Always bad when they tell me to look at the feeds," he ruminated. "See this? Fire. Explosions. Days like this make me want to find a nice, quiet cubicle and stay busy with something else."

"Which is why you quit years ago."

Jim touched the small screen to start the audio-visual display. "—Polar News, reporting a nuclear detonation in the vicinity of the Tokyo Starport," the evening news anchor narrated as full-color photography of a shattered city skyline leaped in to the center of the wireless tablet. "Japanese government officials confirm that automated regional air defenses went into action 13 minutes ago in an effort to shoot down what was believed to be incoming intermediate-range ballistic missiles."

Cook showed his screen to the lieutenant. "Even if it was just a near miss, they're out of action. Death toll will be in the thousands. Gonna take years to decontaminate the place before they can use it again."

"What does this mean for you?" Latham wondered without taking his eyes off the device, "I mean, how does this affect you—Kodiak. Alaska. Us."

The administrator turned off his computer and gave it to the ashen-faced woman who was waiting nearby. "There weren't that many starports to begin with," he related. "The others were knocked out early in this thing they call a war. Bankruptcy got what the cruise missiles didn't."

Jim tugged on his uncomfortable tie. "New Mexico was taken over by the Feds last year. FAA wisdom shut them down two months ago. All their people and transferable systems have been scattered to federal installations around the country. Until 14 minutes ago, that left Kodiak and Tokyo."

"What about Houston?"

Jim laughed cantankerously. "It *was* still under construction when the shooting started," he snorted. "The Feds took their people and equipment two years ago. You know what that means? Kodiak is the only operational starport on friendly soil."

"No allies?"

Jim shook his head "The U.K. site is still under construction. Effort abandoned last year. A few more places like that. Can't remember all of them."

Latham checked his own digital wristwatch. "What are you up against?"

"Baikonur is Russian," Cook recited, "Jiuquan is Chinese. Taiquan doesn't count because it's just a rocket launch facility. Can't do half of what we're capable of. Their upgrades won't be finished for at least five more years, assuming we allow them to happen at all."

The lieutenant touched the radio on his belt. "How would you like to proceed?" he asked. "I'm sure the president will understand if—"

Kelly Haines waved to get Jim's attention. "Lead is in the lecture hall. Route secure. You can go now."

Jim pointed at his watch, "Round 'em up." He put one hand on Latham's shoulder and pointed while his entourage began to board the waiting elevators. "A wise man has recently told me that we should work with what we have. See the nice lady over the sidearm and suitcase?"

"Communications?"

Jim smiled. "My number two on Kodiak is having a heartburn moment right now," he chuckled. "Lotta pain. She's probably got people scattering in all directions."

Latham's gaze returned to the telecom briefcase.

Jim eyed his watch again. "They're not going to use that hotline until they've run their bases and filled out all the emergency situation check lists that I may have saddled them with just for moments like this."

A guard appeared in his field of view carrying his satchel. "Sir, this was left unattended."

Jim glanced at the chair where he'd put his briefcase. "Somebody must've picked it up when I wasn't looking." He took the luggage from the man, who then departed.

"We should go," Latham said, motioning to an empty elevator car that his aide was holding for them.

Jim shifted his load from one hand to the other as they entered the waiting elevator.

Haines appeared at his side with two large guards close behind. "I'll take that," she offered with her free hand.

"Mouse went for the cheese."

"I'll have it looked at," she affirmed, taking his briefcase.

Cook leaned in close. "No change in routine until Latham can make an arrest."

"I know the drill," Kelly protested.

"So did the person you replaced."

She turned to her subordinates. "You and you. With him. Now!"

Latham moved out of the way as both men filled the elevator car with their bulk. Haines walked away with her boss's property casually slung.

"Have you got a threat?" the officer asked as the elevator doors closed. "Is there something I should tell my people?"

Jim tugged at his suit coat. "You saw what I saw. That means you know what I know. So. Let's go. I've got a room full of skeptics waiting for me."

Minutes later, Cook found himself in the rear of the auditorium, waiting to be introduced. "No calls from the starport," he noted while strategizing with his lead PR assistant. "That means the situation is under control. So, I'm going out there."

"Right," the aide acknowledged while making notes on an electronic tablet.

Jim handed over his own small computer. "Be sure to leave this where somebody can find it. They won't need more than a few seconds to see what's on it."

"It's junk."

"Misdirection," he nodded.

"You really think this'll work?"

Jim shrugged while handing her the pad. "No. Enemy agents are hard to predict. You're probably wasting your time."

"Why are they going to waste *their* time?" the secretary argued.

Jim didn't answer. He turned to face Kelly Haines as she appeared. "There you are! Tokyo won't affect us for twelve hours. It's not going to surprise me if your secured link goes off while I'm on stage. Just take a message. Be the first person I talk to when this is over. Got it? Don't be polite. Shove to the front of the line, if there is one."

"Yes, sir!"

"You're on," Lieutenant Latham indicated as the audience applauded.

Jim took a deep breath and let it out melodramatically before walking casually out of the wings, on to the stage where he shook the campus president's hand. "We have to stop meeting like this," he grinned, approaching a lectern.

The podium's wireless microphone system electronically adjusted to broadcast his voice throughout the large assembly hall. Out of habit, he put one hand on a ridge of worn multimedia controls and the other on the outer edge of the pedestal.

"Good evening," he began. "My name is Jim Cook. I'm the Senior Administrator for the Kodiak Starport. It's a title that sounds a bit old fashioned because they won't let me change it. Dates back to the old-old days, when NASA started with a just a few pilots crazy enough to ride rockets into low orbit."

He cleared his throat. "I'm in charge. That's what they tell me. The chain of command that answers when I call currently consists of a deputy administrator, five on-site department heads, and three more who are located elsewhere."

A holographic display coalesced into view as he spoke. Early images of the space launch complex appeared and faded in chronological order. "Kodiak Starport is one of the best known places in Alaska. It started in the late 1990s as a joint venture between the private sector and the State of Alaska. Everything we are known for today comes from that humble beginning."

He paused. "Our parent company is Shadow Fusion Enterprises. Ticker symbol SHFE. I wouldn't be surprised if some of you or your parents are stockholders."

A slow-moving montage of photos and video clips played through a transparent hologram over his head. "As you know, there has been some trouble with the neighbors," he explained while headlines and sound bites paraded overhead, visually summarizing wins and losses, "We're not the only ones who tasted modern war."

Cook spent several minutes explaining the layout of an elaborate map of the 3,000-acre facility as its image rotated slowly. "Wartime necessity has swelled our employment to 5,000. As the gateway to the future that we like to call ourselves, it has become necessary to hire some guards and lock the doors. You know how it is. Protect the family silver and keep the other guy's dog off our lawn. That sort of thing."

He shifted his stance and, without pausing, selected a new series of images to run. "All of us are still getting over the loss of our first space station. It's been 23 and a half months. Feels like it just happened. *Gold Rush* would've been a real asset to the Alaskan economy. Look. Just hold on a minute." He gestured. "I see all the questions you're texting."

Jim turned off the holographic projector so the audience would have nothing else to look at. "Okay. Here it is. There was a strategic weapon onboard *Gold Rush*. I gave the go-ahead, so I may as well have put it there with my own two hands," he sighed. "I won't apologize for it, either. We acted with full Presidential authority. I sat through ten months of Congressional hearings while the rest of you watched me sit through ten months of Congressional hearings. No convictions. No jail time. I'm clean.

"We made a hard choice. The fact is that you're watching this war on television. There are no hostile forces on Alaskan soil. Those of you who are learning Chinese in a classroom do so by choice, rather than by necessity.

"I see all those questions about what's in the news," he asserted, "Fact is, I'm standing here now because I want to make a point. Many of you would be expect me to end my talk early because of what has just happened in Japan. No."

He stepped away from the podium, motioning with one hand. "Let's put all that aside. You've got a future to think about. So do we. A starport—any starport—is more than a place for business. It's a nexus for potential. A real-world starting point for great things."

Murmurs from the crowd caused him to raise his voice. "Thirty-five years from this moment, one of you might be the senior administrator for the Kodiak Starport. That means you'll have what used to be my job.

"Think about that!" he suggested loudly. "One of you sitting in this audience, right now, might be the person who stands on this very spot! Your speech is going to be a lot different than mine because times will have changed. You'll have new challenges to deal with."

The mood of many onlookers improved as Cook continued. "Necessity dictates action," he philosophized. "Being a gateway to the future means we hold that door open, through good times and bad. We keep it open, no matter what happens around us."

Voices hushed. Jim took a step to his right. "The neutrality that some of you want to make a case for does not exist. We can't sit this out. The future we want will not build itself. Many of the tools we need to achieve spaceflight will be essential to the cleanup of our polluted environment."

Heads turned. "Every problem has a fix," the administrator claimed. "Some of those solutions come in the form of new jobs. Some include spaceflight. Astronauts. Pilots. Mission specialists. What they fly and when they do it is still being negotiated, but we are working on it."

Jim paused for cheers and applause. "As frosty cool as that is, we're also going to need biologists, ecologists, fuel handlers, electricians, and service providers in fields you never heard of, to do all the little things that nobody will ever see."

Cook let his arms fall to a more conversational pose. "Droughts and famines are affecting large parts of the world. As you know, the containment lake that held arsenic water for the Small Rock mine failed two years ago. That toxic release is now harming fisheries in Bristol Bay. We're doing our part to deal with it, as any major in-state employer would."

Hands went up. Questions were shouted. "Thanks for letting me veer off topic." He bowed, as if taking everyone in to his private confidence. "That's all the time they had me scheduled for," he indicated by pointing at a large digital clock on a far wall, "Please think about what I said while you're on vacation. Many of you graduate in the spring. Times change and there will always be another crisis. I'd like you to help us keep that gateway to the future open for the next generation of problem solvers."

* * *

Jim was met by Kelly Haines as he strode off stage.

"Nothing," she informed him.

"Let's call that the first miracle of the night," he declared.

"What's the second?"

He pointed in the direction of a hundred students who were leaving the auditorium. "Go to this dinner and say good things about them to a room full of people who wouldn't want to be them just now."

"Which ought to be another tub-thumper," Governor Sheldon Wheeler's voice encouraged.

Jim turned to see the younger man standing feet away, flanked by a pair of plain clothed State Troopers. "Well. You're not supposed to be here." He blinked. "But, since you are—"

"My flight to Juneau was diverted when Tokyo happened," Wheeler explained while tugging at his formal attire. "I'd like to sit in on your dinner with the Board of Regents. Before we do, though, I think we ought to have a few words behind closed doors."

"About what?"

"Something for the history books," Sheldon replied, his voice strained.

Cooked turned to Latham. "I need a room."

"Come," the lieutenant motioned earnestly while giving orders through his radio.

The administrator and key members of his team followed in single file through a back stage door, down a dark corridor, through a maintenance room, into a large open area filled with modular office furniture. Cook's entourage was tailed by Governor Wheeler and several of his most trusted executives.

"Doors over there and there are locked," Latham explained. "Nobody comes in unless you open one of them from this side. I'll be outside if you need me."

Cook waited for both groups to spread out. He found the nearest chair and sat. "Okay. You have our attention. Just tell me one thing. Why are you here?"

The governor's advisors found perches nearby. The well-dressed politician selected a chair and sank in to it. He turned slowly. "Seriously, I was on my way home for Christmas with the family. You do remember what that's like, don't you? Food. Presents. Not working for just a few hours? Try it some time. You might like it."

Jim laughed, "My wife thinks I staged this war so I can avoid coming home."

Wheeler frowned. "I'm sorry to hear that. Can I ask what your plans are, now that they've paved Tokyo?"

"I'm not sure this is the place for that."

Sheldon remained cordial despite his worsening mood. "This is a little off the cuff," he confessed. "I'm just making the most of a situation. You're here. I'm here. Talk. Anything you can say to me about what comes next should be heard by everyone in this room, so that we can all be on the same page."

"We're going to use Nanook," Cook told him flatly.

Sheldon became visibly reticent. "I'm not—"

"I am!" Jim stood up, "You said it yourself. They paved Tokyo! Wrecked it! Burned it to a cinder and scattered the ashes. The story I saw mentioned something about regional air defenses, which means the attack came in over a monitored trajectory. Our neighbors in Beijing wanted us—Kodiak Starport—to know who did that. It's their way of saying we're next if we don't shut up and play nice. That's why we've got to respond with something more than a phone call to Washington asking for help!"

The governor crossed his legs in an effort to remain seated. "Don't sell diplomacy short," he rebuked. "The international community won't stand for what they've just seen. It'll take a while, but they will respond!"

The administrator stepped away from his chair and surveyed the room. "I suppose you had to ask," he said after looking at the faces around him. "Why hasn't anyone called me?"

Wheeler stood up slowly. "I think opinions are divided," he speculated candidly. "Nobody said anything to me that would hold up in court. Bottom line is, they won't cover for you again. State Department hinted that the President would look favorably on anything 'positive' you did, if it didn't—"

"Yeah," Cook cringed. "Heard that one before. What do *you* say?"

The politician smoothed out his tie. "We were talking," he waved to indicate his advisors. "I've got a whole state to think about and D.C. is on the other side of the world. Whatever they do will be based on what this looks like from where they sit."

"How do I convince you that this is a local problem?"

Sheldon moved his chair aside. "I can be very hard to find when I want to be," he hinted. "A lot of the governors do it these days."

"Must be nice," Jim chuckled.

"It could be, for you," Wheeler proposed. "Don't answer some e-mail. Plead hotline failure to slow reporting with some agencies. Leave the rest to me. Between your people and mine, there might be a week's worth of wiggle room in there for you do to something. Whatever that is, I will never—*ever*—know about it."

The starport boss pivoted to confer with his communications director. "I see what he means. We can't be arrested or told to stop if they can't talk to us. What else would we need?"

"A more proactive statement of some kind would help," the man decided after some thought. "Show of solidarity. Something a rep from the governor's office can respond to for the next few days, while he's being hard to find."

"I've got a banquet hall filled with old guys waiting to see me hand over a letter that promises big money." Jim brainstormed. "Could we arrange to make that statement after the event? Immediately?"

"There's already enough media here to cover it," one of Wheeler's people offered.

The administrator looked at his watch. "Sheldon, this would be our cue to leave. Let these guys kill a goat or whatever it is they do to write a script. We'll surprise the regents with yourself as an unexpected guest and do that press conference afterward. Should be fun."

CHAPTER THREE

International reaction to the destruction of Japan's starport was swift and reproachful. Regional surveillance, provided by airborne sensor platforms, was rapidly collected and analyzed while commentators summarized what happened through radio and television.

"Weather patterns are likely to disperse fallout…"

"Fire and ambulance services are overwhelmed."

"—no more allied space launch capacity."

* * *

The one-kiloton airburst, delivered by a missile moderately capable of avoiding military radar emissions, had slipped through Japanese air defenses on a very sharp trajectory. Software-assisted countermeasures came into effect as the threat was detected and categorized. Orders were sent to computer-controlled short-range missile batteries in multiple provinces.

The intruding payload entered and exited these predefined defense zones at supersonic speeds, reaching its activation point as defensive weapons throughout the region failed to intercept the attack.

The resulting pressure waves crushed Tokyo Starport's surface-level facilities. A combination of atmospheric effects, resulting from overpressure and tectonic activity, ruptured pipe and conduit systems in a nine-mile radius. Ignition of volatile chemicals and stored fuel caused a firestorm that incinerated power management infrastructure in a four-mile radius from the epicenter of the explosion.

The electromagnetic pulse from the nuclear airburst itself wreaked havoc with electronic systems in a 12-mile radius. Underground command-and-control networks attempting to prevent the attack reacted to new inputs. Protected computers, encrypted programs, and hardened sensors located throughout the region agreed that the unthinkable had happened.

Launch and trajectory analysis, conducted by a series of government-funded supercomputers prepared for just such scenarios, satisfied political concerns. The nature and source of the attack was validated based on more than 200 predefined characteristics intended to eliminate the potential for accidental misclassification.

Human operators in shielded bunkers were asked for permission to unleash Japan's nuclear response against Chinese targets. Elected representatives and civil servants were ordered to leave vulnerable cities. Senior leaders were presented with options while being ushered to secured installations.

Pre-recorded emergency alert messages, warning citizens about the dangers of fallout and sudden electrical power loss, were transmitted through remaining radio, television, and internet providers.

* * *

"I have no idea what the Japanese response will be," Jim lied when asked during the banquet with university executives. "We're all feeling the loss of satellite capacity just now. Debris is falling faster than many predicted. Early efforts to clear the most desirable low orbit pathways have been quite successful."

Cook raised his wine glass in the awkward silence. "We're not the only ones to deploy robots up there. Japan, Russia, and China have been sending unmanned platforms upstairs to give the larger pieces a push into decaying orbits, just like we have."

He shrugged when the room remained silent. "I know what you're thinking, and your guess is as good as mine. Who goes first? China may have already done it. We should assume there are a few birds up there in geosynchronous, away from the worst of the worst debris clouds, looking down at everything we do."

"Does that mean our enemies have significant communications?" somebody asked.

"No," Jim theorized, "not in the way you mean. Every satellite in low orbit was destroyed. I'm not exaggerating. I mean all of them, which is to say there are no more, nor will there be for quite some time, because of the trash that blocks the better flightpaths. This event has crippled worldwide civilization in ways that are now scaring the average person, who can't get a good internet connection or make a reliable phone call as easily as he used to. I'm sure everyone in this room has experienced some of that anxiety."

He put his glass down softly as heads turned. "For those of you who aren't paying attention, let me be a little more reassuring. There are still a few spy satellites and telecom birds in high orbit. They aren't so reliable at the moment, due to all that wreckage blocking what they can see. That trash also interferes with the signals they send back to Earth. This means," he added for dramatic effect, "that the major powers still have some capacity to see and hear regionally, though no longer globally."

"How do we come back from this?" a worried voice asked.

Cook spread his hands. "Worldwide broadband took decades to develop. Partial restoration may require ten years to replace, if we can put a stop to hostilities long enough to build and orbit new systems. As long as hostilities remain in effect," he emphasized with a claw-like gesture, "any satellite that sends or receives large amounts of traffic will stand out like a neon sign at midnight. It would be vulnerable to detection, which means, eventually, it *will* be shot down."

"Be more specific," Governor Wheeler prompted from his seat at a nearby table filled with senior academics. "How is Kodiak Starport being watched?"

The administrator grimaced. "Any satellites in space right now, this very second, are look-and-listen systems with line-of-sight transmitters synched to ground stations or ships at sea that don't move around very much. They'll be sending tight data streams. That's 'limited surveillance' to you and me. Just enough to keep an eye on certain parts of the world, which would include our little slice of heaven."

* * *

Millions of men, women, and children left Tokyo prefecture as police, fire, and ambulance units attempted to reach the shattered starport. Confusion became panic when gray ash fell on orderly processions that were milling through carefully prearranged control points. Evacuees stampeded when they believed that radioactive particulates were showering down upon them.

Digital cameras throughout the stricken city streamed wireless images to dozens of infotainment networks around the world. Distant broadcasters provided lurid voice-over commentary as subscribers watched the carnage unfold.

"—happening too fast for words."

"Police barricades are falling and riot lines are not holding!"

"Look at 'em go! It's out of control!"

* * *

Tensions rose throughout the Kodiak Starport's new underground mission control complex. Area clocks indicated 9:22 p.m. as the night shift struggled to bring recently assembled components online.

"Only a matter of time until they come for us," somebody murmured.

"Was their ABM system online? I think ours is better than theirs."

Faces turned from exposed circuit boards and flashing screens while software ran through tedious diagnostics. Men and women wearing white shirts featuring a big blue starport logo splashed across the backs paused to stare at high-mounted monitors around the cavernous room.

Lurid newsfeed continued to blaze from three-dimensional projectors as the technicians worked to make ground-based flight management systems ready for use. Licensed product representatives called for spec checks at irregular intervals as major systems were connected.

Deputy Administrator Raven Frost, dressed in a conservative gray tailored suit, surveyed her surroundings with an experienced eye as she walked from one side of the cavernous room to the other. Her long, dark hair was secured in a bun behind her head. Observant brown eyes saw everything over high cheekbones as she evaluated the progress of each working group. A wireless microphone hung from one ear, allowing her to hear multi-frequency chatter.

"Transmission failed."

"Line check, multiple disconnect."

"Give us a minute to run that down."

Frost made a show of ignoring the news, hoping that others would follow her example when she paused to examine their work. There was a lot more at stake than the unit supervisors were aware of. Insurance company representatives were on-site, looking for any reason at all to deny payment for damages. Adjusters were hoping to use acts of nature or the failings of starport employees as justifications for not paying.

* * *

"It's been a hallmark of the University of Alaska system for decades that we can overcome adversity," the campus president concluded. "Our gathering this evening proves that point, again. As we observe the holiday break, I'd like to voice the gratitude of our student body, Board of Regents, and the people of Anchorage when I thank all of you for your generous time and support."

Jim made his way through the crowd, shaking hands as he reached the nearest exit. He was met by a uniformed starport guard in the hallway.

"Took the bait," the man whispered.

Jim turned in his tracks. "Who was it?" he inquired while scanning the faces around him as they passed by.

"Latham's aide," the former soldier grunted. "We saw it on three different cameras. He was fast."

"Sorry to hear that," Jim sighed.

"Takes all kinds," the protector decided.

Cook looked at his watch before he started walking. Armed guards gathered around him as he moved. "Coordinate with Latham. This is his turf, so let him have the collar. It'll be one less thing for us to do. Ask the Governor to meet me in the back room. Then, find Haines. I want the big phone."

* * *

News and infotainment organizations across the State of Alaska prepared to cover the post-banquet press conference as the unexpected participation of Governor Sheldon Wheeler was announced. Television and radio stations scrambled to free up air time for the event when 'unnamed sources' hinted through social media that the governor and a high-ranking starport spokesperson would be making a statement concerning recent happenings in Japan.

* * *

Raven went to the central administrator's dais when she received an incoming call on a secured line. Sitting in a high-backed swivel chair, she used a touchscreen to activate recently modernized telecom controls.

"Hello from Anchorage," Jim announced in her ear.

"Wasn't expecting to hear from you," she replied calmly while scanning news headlines with sudden interest.

"I'm not checking on you," Jim interrupted. "That thing we talked about is happening."

Frost remained outwardly composed, though she was aware of the implications. "You know what my thoughts are. None of us are safe. You're at the top, so they'll come for you first. We've planned for this."

Jim paused. "It's your sunny disposition. That's why you're on a fast track."

"You picked me to be a realist," she reminded him.

"So I did," he mumbled, "What was I thinking? All right, then. Let's show them what they expect to see."

"It's got to look real," Raven maintained.

"Please don't lecture me about deception," he chided. "I've broken more laws and violated more treaties than you will live to see future presidents make."

* * *

Lieutenant Latham eyed a tiny black capsule at the end of a pair of tweezers when it was shown to him by one of Cook's uniformed specialists. "This is a very small robot. He's bashful right now because we caught him. Its job is to hide in small spaces, programmed to release a nerve agent. We believe there is just enough poison to kill everyone in the passenger compartment of the aircraft we arrived in."

"My officer did this?" Latham scowled.

"It's okay," Jim consoled from just a few paces away. "You had no way of knowing. This is…um…just another part of my job. Such fun."

"What do you need?"

Jim looked around the large room, at the inquisitive faces staring back at him. "It's a ticklish moment. Keep an eye on your rogue element. The Governor and I will dazzle the press with our brilliance. Then, we're going to leave as publicly as we can. You pick up the pieces and play hero when we're gone."

"With that?" Latham nodded at the tiny robot.

The expert waggled his tweezers. "There's a solid fingerprint on this linking your man to the crime. Add that to your own security video and you've got him."

"Why give us the credit?" Latham wondered.

Jim leaned in with a broad smile. "My wife keeps telling me to share. It's Christmas. We don't have time for gift wrapping, but you get the idea. He's all yours."

"Gotta go," a secretary signaled.

"Right." Cook clapped the officer on one shoulder, "That little robot is mine. I've got something special in mind. We've already made sure you have a copy of the fingerprint for the arrest warrant. That alright with you?"

* * *

News organizations prepared to receive live feed from the Anchorage campus as officials from the University of Alaska opened the internationally televised press conference by making a few brief remarks.

Attendance was light. The spacious lobby echoed with voices as each speaker approached a portable podium festooned with wireless microphones.

Wheeler surveyed the audience and the assembled reporters on the far side of a velvet rope line. He didn't like the prepared remarks his team had given him.

"No young reporters," he complained quietly.

Cook paid more attention to the audience. Wheeler's observation became more apparent as he looked from left to right. "They're all in school or wearing a uniform," he lamented, stating the obvious.

"This has to stop," the Governor protested.

"Workin' on it," Jim growled.

* * *

"We have ours and they have theirs," Ivan explained while zipping his parka. He strolled down a long cold dimly-lit walkway high above an underground workshop with Norman just a few paces behind. A long, teardrop-shaped fuselage with broad wings and tapered nose sat on an empty concrete floor below.

Norman stared in awe. The starport's version of a military space plane was visible in soft area lighting. A pair of vertical fins jutted from the rear like shark fins. "Not very big," he muttered, cramming both hands in his coat pockets.

"Every ton counts," Gallagher nodded, "Flat as a pancake, so it'll go through the air like a knife. Sources tell me the Chinese model is pretty much the same."

"No visible canopy," Ahgupuk observed while scratching his chin, "Wouldn't be. Too many structural issues. I assume it's a scramjet. Would I be right?"

"Can't say," Ivan explained without taking his eyes off the aerospace marvel. "I have it from people I trust that this beast killed a dozen test pilots."

"Airframe or avionics?"

"Related failures," the bald man intoned solemnly. "It's too unstable at high speed. No human really flies a thing like this. You're just an add-on that helps the computers when they're having a rare moment of stupid."

"Any chance we could—"

"No," the agitated man asserted. "This is as close as we get. Soak it up. Take it all in. We're out of here in 30 seconds."

"How are the pilots selected? Have they seen combat?"

"Don't know," Ivan mumbled.

"What's the training plan?"

Gallagher walked away. His cane struck the floor at regular intervals. "Forget about it. You're never going to meet 'em. They're never going to meet you or know your name. Not for any reason."

Ahgupuk paused for a last look at the space plane. "Lucky to be here," he sighed.

"Merry Christmas—for sure!" Ivan laughed while he sauntered. "Wouldn't want to be on the receiving end of that package."

Norman followed his benefactor out of the hangar. "When do they fly?"

"This is real knock-down, drag-out war," Gallagher ruminated as they approached an open elevator. "None of that graduated, slow boil, anti-terrorism stuff. Yes. They're going to fly. When? Don't know."

* * *

The starport administrator's assumption that there *must* be spy satellites in low orbit was a widely held belief among the war planners of all combatant nations. Their worries were unfounded, though none of their intelligence services had any way of determining that. Every effort to put observation platforms into a temporary low altitude position had been terminated in the study phase of each project for logistical reasons.

* * *

Governor Wheeler approached the podium. He steadied himself and waited for his notes to appear on a nearby teleprompter. “Alaskans are resourceful,” he began with his customary optimism. “It’s in our nature to overcome what seems like impossible odds. Extreme temperatures and long distances over difficult terrain are just some of what we face every day.”

Sheldon’s remarks were met with approval. “There’s more at stake than Alaska’s homegrown aerospace industry,” he emphasized to the nearest camera as if it were a person who needed convincing. “Our future as a species is at risk. What you’ve just seen in Tokyo was a look at our future, if we continue to make bad choices. That’s got to stop. Here. Now. Or the consequences could be…unthinkable.”

“I have to agree with Governor Wheeler,” Jim said supportively when it was his turn to address the reporters. “Civilization, as we know it, is in crisis. The oceans are depleted. Droughts are common on every continent. Extreme weather is just a symptom of our problems. Now, there’s this.”

He gestured brazenly. “D’you people realize this is the third time Japan has been nuked? That’s a pretty grim statistic, even if you can get past what happened at Fukushima. Fact is, we are—all of us—in a bad place.”

The crowd went silent. Jim raked the front row with bitter scorn. “Don’t give me that look. I know what I said. Look, here’s the thing,” he complained while folding his hands on the narrow podium. “We can fix this. There *is* still time.”

“How?” somebody queried.

"Good question." Cook bent soberly. "This one doesn't come with an easy answer. A few hours ago, I was telling the students here that we've still got to invent many of the tools they need to make a better future. That's the truth. Part of that invention process will require a functioning starport."

He pointed. "Spaceflight isn't a cure for everything that's wrong on planet Earth, but it can help. Some of what we need isn't at the bottom of the ocean or under a mountain. It's out there, in our solar system. Orbiting our planets. All we have to do is stop killing each other long enough to bring it back here and use it wisely."

"How do you keep the Kodiak Starport open for business?" another voice asked.

"Very carefully," Jim smirked.

"I've heard rumors about aerospace fighters," a Fairbanks reporter probed.

"American or Chinese?" Cook asked rhetorically.

"Yours."

Jim shrugged. "Spaceflight is our business. Anyone who had such technology would use it, eventually."

"Are you saying that you *do* have—"

"Not for offensive purposes," Cook asserted loudly. "That sort of decision-making is left to sovereign governments, as part of international law."

The admission stunned everyone in the room with its implications. Commentators who were broadcasting live had similar reactions.

Jim turned to face Sheldon with a jaunty gesture. "Follow *that*, if you can."

* * *

Ground crews worked through final checks under bright lights inside underground hangars at China's Jiuquan starport. Fuel and ordnance loading was finished while instruments and safety systems were inspected.

Senior pilots with combat experience in terrestrial jet fighters were driven to the planes. State-approved media representatives followed at a respectful distance with handheld cameras to record the event for later broadcast. Each aviator was clad in a vacuum suit that wasn't much different than the type worn by the nation's astronauts.

Dark sun visors were pulled down on bulbous helmets to hide faces. Squadron patches, military emblems, and national insignia adorned the outer shell of their adapted suits. No name tags or rank insignia were visible as they climbed ladders to enter cockpits through clamshell apertures in the upper hull of each airframe. Surviving the mission guaranteed career advancement and the commercial opportunity to become household names throughout China and around the world.

* * *

Governor Wheeler's response to the revelation of armed spacecraft at the Kodiak Starport caused him to be the first American politician on record. "Recent events have put us in a difficult position," he told the nearest camera. "You heard what Mr. Cook had to say. We've got to be creative."

"Did you know this?" a correspondent inquired.

"First I've heard of it," Sheldon lied, "though I don't disapprove. Naturally, our state legislature will have questions."

"Why would that be necessary?" the man speculated.

Wheeler shrugged. "We're in a gray area," he appeared to concede. "This is my first war. We have some guidance from Washington. Some. A little bit."

On impulse, he reached into his coat pocket for a wireless phone. "Look at this," he insisted while brandishing the device. "We've all got one. Most of 'em aren't very useful right now."

The politician dropped his phone. It landed on the floor between his polished shoes with a hollow thud. "That's us in another decade if we don't stop this decline, or whatever you'd like to call it. We've got more oil and gas than our grandparents ever thought possible. Too bad we can't eat it."

Photographers were divided. Some leaned over to get close-up shots of the Governor's discarded cell phone. Others focused on his concerned expression.

"We *do* make the future we want to live in," Sheldon emphasized. "My early predecessors did some of that with an oil pipeline and reforms to fishing and tourism that put us on the map. Natural gas gave us a boost. Now, it's my turn to make a contribution. Here. Now. I'm giving the Kodiak Starport my full support."

* * *

Cook enjoyed gossiping with the campus cop after the press conference. It was 10:06 p.m.

"You're sure about that?" Lieutenant Latham said doubtfully inside the crowded elevator.

"What news programs do you watch?" Jim asked as he and his security detail made their way to the roof.

"WNN," Latham admitted.

Jim bobbed his head. "Look at our Starport News some time. You might see something."

"All networks are crud," the former cop swore.

"That's my brand you're talking about," Jim objected. "We're a lot of things, but crud isn't one of them. Beatrice Brown doesn't do crud."

"Who?"

"Never mind," Cook snapped as the lift came to a stop. "China is moving on more than one front. They've been pressuring the Russians for months now about resources in the Far East. Off and on for the last decade, if you want to be technical about it."

Armed guards walked off the elevator and spread out. Jim brushed at his suit. "It's in the news. What you don't hear about is all the diplomatic pitter-patter of expensive shoes going between Moscow and Beijing. Trust me. It's only a matter of time until the dragon decides to see what a bear tastes like."

The officer followed Cook off the elevator when it was their turn to exit. "They seem rather cozy at the moment," he observed.

"Friends close and enemies closer."

Jim made his way across the lounge quickly, stopping to take his briefcase from Kelly Haines, who held it out to him. "Call Raven," he told her while checking his grip. "Tell her what you see, when you see it. She may have questions."

"How many more bad eggs do you think we have?" Latham asked Haines.

"No way to be sure," she empathized. "Everybody thinks we're leaving by air. You or one of your people would have come up here with us. Somebody in your command post is watching us right now through this building's camera system."

Jim went outside on to the brightly lit landing pad, flanked by a pair of guards. He approached a pilotless VTOL. It sat motionless in the center of the landing pad with a cargo door open. He slid his briefcase in through an open cargo door. It glided effortlessly on the carpeted floor. Cameras on and in the aircraft allowed starport technicians more than 600 miles away to see his every move as he surveyed the well-appointed interior. "What a waste," he grumbled as he closed the door.

Cook walked back inside as engines on the unmanned aircraft began to spin up. He stopped halfway across the helipad to watch the VTOL lift off in a spray of ice and snow. Troubling thoughts were hard to ignore. Espionage and sabotage were now a part of his job in ways that past starport managers could never have imagined.

"Was that necessary?" Latham wondered while peering through a plate glass window.

"All for show," the executive explained as he walked back inside.

Haines gave him a wireless handset. "Somebody in this town is expecting us to leave the same way we came in. They might activate some sort of unpredictable backup plan if we don't play along."

"Clever," Latham acknowledged as the VTOL's running lights vanished from sight.

Jim swung his arms as the radio in his hand chirped. "I've never been murdered. My wife has threatened to do it a few times. This'll be a new experience."

He shuffled over to Haines. "Are we ready?"

She nodded. "Convoy is waiting. Tell me where we're going so I can inform the State Troopers."

"Corporate," Cook decided. "Take me to company headquarters. We'll overnight there and find our way home in the morning."

"What about the Governor?"

Jim consulted his watch. "He's got an official motorcade. They'll be gone before we get downstairs. Somebody make sure the press finds Latham."

The officer laughed. "No need. UAA has its own media machine. They'll milk this for all it's worth."

Cook paused while his transport disappeared over the horizon. "All right then," he smiled while offering his hand to the officer. "Good luck with being famous for a day. Now, if you'll excuse me, I'm about to be killed by enemy sabotage."

Jim's trailing guards conferred with Latham about the starport entourage's departure plans for several minutes before the administrator was escorted downstairs through a system of secured maintenance corridors and freight elevators.

Latham conferred with his superiors by radio as they travelled. He held a door open as the rapidly moving group emerged into the cold night. "You'll have an escort to the edge of campus," he informed Cook. "State Troopers will pick you up on Lake Otis Parkway and escort you all the way downtown. You're good to go."

Jim looked up and down the row of dark blue four-wheel drive vehicles that waited for him. Each of the easily identifiable executive transports was flanked by armed starport guards, who stood quietly in the falling snow. Engines idled. Radios chattered.

"Did you hear my speech this evening?"

"I did," Latham confirmed.

The starport boss gestured at the building his staffers were shuffling out of. "That gateway to the future I mentioned has a lot of moving parts. Rockets and classrooms are just some of what it takes to keep the whole thing going."

"Figured as much," the cop agreed while brushing snow off the brim of his hat.

"Keep up the good work!" Jim encouraged before walking away.

CHAPTER FOUR

American war planners adapted to the loss of Tokyo's starport after an evaluation of all the facts. Human analysts worked with computers that presented updated post-damage assessments on a minute-by-minute basis.

Sophisticated A.I.'s generated best-case scenarios that were catalogued and prioritized before being sent to Cabinet-level intermediaries. The most productive actions that could yield efficient military or diplomatic outcomes were quietly brought to the executive branch.

* * *

"Has it really come to this?" the President asked just after 2:10 a.m. local time.

"It's far worse than the mainstream media thinks it is," an intelligence expert sighed. "Indicators are that Tokyo Starport and some of the city is a total loss. Casualties will be counted into the millions. All that comes out in the wash real soon. Hours."

The chief executive rubbed his chin. "In any other situation, we'd be using that time constructively."

"This isn't any normal situation," a representative from the Army dissented. "We're blind without satellites. Airborne reconnaissance does have limits. That means no verification of any handshake you could make through a diplomatic hotline."

"There *is* an opportunity here," an Air Force general disagreed from where he sat. "If Kodiak does what we expect them to, there will be a momentary break in the action while the opposition reconsiders. That's your chance to negotiate."

Men and women around the Oval Office looked at each other.

"Any pause would be welcome," a Navy admiral offered. "They have six carrier battle groups. One of them is in port right now. The other four are at sea, trying to engage us. Yes, we have four carriers. No, they aren't fully supported. We can fight, and we will, but I feel obliged to point out that we're also running out of room to parley. At the very least, Kodiak's action may give us a chance to catch our breath long enough to refit our own carriers."

The second term President looked at the printed page rustling between his fingers. "You're asking me to let a multinational corporation off the leash. Suppose we can't bring them back in to the fold?"

"You think they'd go rogue?" the chief of staff guessed from his chair.

An intelligence expert coughed. "All starports are powers to be reckoned with. Kodiak, in particular, has a history of independent action. As a conglomerate, they have a lot to protect. That includes one-of-a-kind resources that can't be moved. They might stand down, if threatened with what just happened to Japan."

"That's not how this management team does things," the senior Army officer reminded his colleagues.

A lawyer from the Justice Department crossed his legs and frowned. "Doesn't matter what they do. We've already given them immunity for past activities. You can't do that again. I suggest—"

"You're all making sense," the President interrupted, "Let's give Mr. Cook some time to work his magic. What's the word from Japan?"

A quiet woman from the State Department folded her hands. "As expected, their Prime Minister is under a lot of pressure to pull the nuclear trigger. He's going along with our request for a delayed response, which means we owe him a favor."

"Good," the President relaxed, "Schedule a block of air time in 24 hours. If this is anything like the *Gold Rush* incident, we'll have some explaining to do," he said worriedly, dropping the page on his desk. "Is there anything else I should know?"

* * *

Sirens wailed to order evacuation of the launch apron as fueling lines were disconnected. The absence of an obvious bubble canopy or cockpit windscreen on any of the aircraft convinced some of the technicians they were preparing drones for action.

Teardrop silhouettes wrapped in black radar absorbent composites with variable geometry wings taxied for takeoff on retractable landing gears. Single vertical stabilizers and flat, rounded noses gave each aerospace vehicle the appearance of an aquatic shark. Moments later, the three modular multirole airframes roared down five-mile lengths of individually shielded underground runway on rocket sleds, erupting into the midday sky at speeds in excess of 600 miles per hour. Scramjets inside each stealthy fuselage began to gulp air as solid rockets ignited, pushing each Type 1000 craft through the sound barrier in a matter of minutes.

Spent boosters fell away with a jarring thud as the pilots reacted enthusiastically to the adrenaline rush provoked by such an extreme takeoff. Surveillance satellites still operating in high orbit observed the launch and transmitted partial sensor data to ground stations through clouds of moving debris. Human analysts in several countries evaluating this information classified the exhaust plumes and radar tracks they saw as "strategic rocket activity, target unknown."

* * *

Norman showed his ID card to the secretary while placing his thumb on a sensor. "The deputy wants to see me," he explained. He looked at himself in a reflective surface nearby to see that his appearance was in good order. Thoughts of what he'd recently been made privy to were still fresh in his mind as he brushed at his uniform.

"She's expecting you," the sleepy man relayed for the benefit of a nearby guard.

The excited aviator waited for the reinforced door to slide open. He stepped into the newly constructed administrator's office, perched high above the floor of a busy operations chamber, which could be seen through transparent windows. Muted lighting, dark furnishings, and flickering images on a dozen wall-mounted screens enveloped him as he entered the room.

"Quite the atmosphere."

"It is," Raven asserted from her position behind a long black desk in a high back chair of the same color. "Reminds me of a villain's lair. How are you, Norman?"

"Not sure."

"Did Santa bring you anything good for Christmas?" she asked politely.

Norman liked Jim Cook personally, though he didn't care for the senior administrator's brusque management style. Raven Frost was mild by comparison. Her quiet intercessions helped him get parts and pilots for the starport's old warbirds that he might not otherwise have.

"You asked me here to talk about Santa Claus?"

"Are you satisfied?" she inquired more directly.

"About?" he blinked.

"Things," Raven emphasized sharply.

"Yeah," he nodded vigorously, "Yes. That. I do—I am. Yes."

"You're not going to bother us anymore?"

"No," he declared humbly.

"All right then," she smiled sweetly, "let's move on. I have a new problem."

"Shoot," Norman replied, seating himself in a wide chair.

The deputy administrator folded her hands and sat forward. She touched a control on the desktop to black out the windows around the office. "Bad guys got something close to Mr. Cook. As we speak, his aircraft is on its way by remote control. Nobody's on board. We're waiting for a nerve agent to be released inside the passenger cabin. When that happens, we crash the plane."

"Fake his death," Norman acknowledged.

"This'll be an opening move," she speculated, tracing a manicured finger over the smooth desktop. "They do something. We do something."

He crossed his legs and rubbed his aching knee. "We *are* well defended."

"Better than Tokyo?" she asked worriedly.

Norman laughed. "There is no more tightly controlled airspace on this planet. As good as that is, nobody is safe. Are you asking—"

"No," she interjected tersely, "I'm not. The loss of a starport's management team isn't that much different than the assassination of a national leader."

Ahgupuk sat speechless. He let his feet slide. "Did they decapitate the Tokyo chain of command before wrecking their facilities?"

Raven's expression changed. "The lead administrator and his senior staff were on-site when it happened. None of our encrypted landlines to their underground fallbacks are still active. Nobody answers when we call."

Norman sat up. "I'm using every resource we have. If you'd authorize more fuel, we could increase our patrol radius."

"Do that," she urged. "Bigger show of force. Do it for the next ten days, through the end of the calendar year. Give it a cover story of some kind."

"Atmospheric monitoring to track radiologicals from Tokyo?" he offered.

"Whatever you think is best," Raven replied. "Next order of business. Be in the room when I make the call to air defense. Jim's crash will happen at sea, once we are sure a nerve agent has been released inside the aircraft."

"They go down in the cold winter water," Norman narrated gruesomely. "Nobody can get to him in time. The wreckage sinks before the media moves in."

"Too obvious?"

"No," he said encouragingly. "Splash his VTOL nose first, so the cockpit windscreen implodes. It'll sink like a rock. Just don't crowd the search and rescue when they respond. Let 'em do their job. I'll make sure our response is appropriate for this kind of unexpected tragedy."

"What would that be, exactly?"

"We have two planes ready to go at all times," Norman stated thoughtfully. "I send 'em up as soon as we get the word. Slow orbit until the Coast Guard helicopters arrive. His trailing gunship will see the actual crash, which they'll get on video. Naturally, you will order the pilot to get in low so they can look for survivors. My circling pilots will see that, which they will also have on camera."

Frost rolled back in her chair. "All of it comes back here through official channels, which we gladly share with the media. Everyone who was on that plane will stay in hiding until it's not an advantage anymore."

"It's just on 10:30. I better go."

* * *

Jim Cook's motorcade arrived in downtown Anchorage without incident just after 11 p.m., in spite of dense traffic. All six snow-covered vehicles rolled into the parking garage in single file.

"Alarms have just gone off inside the passenger cabin," Raven told her boss through a secure wireless connection. "Sensor indicates extreme biohazard."

"A hundred miles out to sea and nobody there to save me," Jim chuckled, holding the phone receiver in one hand as his armored transport came to a stop.

"We're still managing the crash," Frost assessed dryly. "Distress call has gone out. They'll put it in the water any second now. I'm hoping for some debris scatter."

"We should've included more expendables," Cook mulled while unbuckling his seatbelt, "Luggage. Food containers. Cold weather gear."

"Nothing to be done about it now," she replied, her tone regretful. "Bird's in the drink. Your gunship escort is coming in to look for survivors. Pilot's on the Coast Guard frequency now. I feel bad. Leaving them in the dark about this—"

"It was the right thing to do," Jim insisted.

"And—oops!"

"What?" he shouted as tired staffers around him got out of the vehicle.

"It sank," Raven sighed heavily through the connection.

Cook glared at the handset in his fist. "Any wreckage?" he demanded.

"Gotta go," she breathed and hung up.

Kelly Haines leaned in through the open door. "Is there a problem?"

Jim looked at the silent phone in his hand. "Not sure." He hesitated before putting the receiver down. "Let's get inside. It's been a long day."

* * *

Cook's entourage was escorted to the spacious ground floor lobby at 11:10 p.m., where he checked in with the building's well-dressed manager.

"A message has just come in for you," the man informed him from behind a jade-covered counter top.

"Odd," Jim observed while reading from a swivel-mounted touch screen. "I've been summoned. At this hour?"

"Who knew we were going to be here?" somebody worried.

Cook finished filling out the paperwork that would authorize expenses for his staff. "Cameras all over the place," he mentioned without looking up. "Somebody upstairs must've seen me walk in. I'd like to know why the Board is in town. Why aren't they off some place warm, talking trash about me?"

"Could be—"

"No speculation!" Jim admonished.

The administrator quietly turned to his secretary. "See that?" He tapped the display. "Marco is chairman of the Board."

"Sounds like there's been a change in leadership," the woman whispered.

Cook looked at his watch. "It's coming up on 11:15. Everybody upstairs and off to bed. No phones or internet. I mean it. *Nothing*. You got me?"

"Full black out," his assistant concurred.

"Any leaks and you're the first person I make unemployed," he threatened. "We're not here. We're all dead until I say otherwise."

"Yes," the woman replied without further comment.

Jim motioned for Haines to come closer. "I need to go upstairs," he told her when she stepped in close. "Short detail. No point in making all of you stay up late."

"Sounds fair," Kelly agreed. "What's this about?"

"How should I know?" he protested. "I was just poisoned. Or drowned. Something like that."

* * *

Reaction to the distress call from Cook's remotely controlled VTOL was immediately predictable. . Coast Guard helicopters and jet aircraft from Kodiak and Sitka were dispatched to the last known location of his downed aircraft.

The senior starport administrator shed his parka before going up 15 stories to the sumptuous quarters and meeting areas reserved for high-ranking company executives. Jim and Kelly entered an elevator with two additional armed guards close behind.

"Your secretary said something about a new Board president," she mentioned as she shifted a brushed aluminum communications case from one hand to the other. "Are you about to be out of work?"

"Wouldn't surprise me."

Kelly listened to the radio chatter in her ear as the elevator doors closed. "Convoy in the garage," she explained. "Ten minutes to gas up. We'll take you home. If it comes to that."

"Thanks," he laughed.

* * *

Reporters, bloggers, and multimedia network representatives who listened to emergency service radio frequencies for any hint of something they regarded as newsworthy were treated to a real-time description of the tragedy as Jim reached the upper floors of the corporate skyscraper.

* * *

"I'm here to see Mister Marco," Jim told a uniformed man sitting behind a small desk in a large waiting room.

The morose guard didn't make eye contact with the agitated executive. He hesitantly examined both Cook's ID card and the man himself before slowly touching a computer screen. "He'd like to see you alone," the unarmed man related softly. "Please go inside."

Jim took a few steps back to confer with his protectors. "Well, now. He's in a good mood. Don't let this inner sanctum stuff fool you. It's all for show. Sorry to make you wait like this. There's another lounge just beyond that door. They're probably going to make *me* wait. This might take a while."

"You're not okay with this?" Kelly surmised.

"Something doesn't feel right," Cook confided.

Both of his armed guards adjusted their loads and scanned the room without moving.

"Not so obvious!" he snapped, "Cameras. I'd be watching me, too."

"What would you like us to do?" Kelly asked.

Jim gave the appearance of careful thought. "You know what? It's late and this is probably nothing. Stay here and be bored."

* * *

Kodiak starport's senior administrator walked into the next room while straightening his tie. Breaking news headlines began to advertise the crash that appeared to have killed him and his management team.

Haines watched him go with some apprehension. Mindful of her recent promotion, she changed channels on her headset radio as the door closed. Turning slowly, she moved away from the sullen attendant while speaking softly. "Team Two, reset and stand by. Team One, reset and come to me. Team Three, prep convoy for short notice departure."

"Is this going to be something?" one of her subordinates questioned.

She looked at her digital wristwatch. "You'd think these guys had better things to do after 11:20 p.m. Boss doesn't like it, so I don't like it."

* * *

The inbound aerospace formation entered low orbit. Its flightpath was intended to guide all three space planes through airspace that was believed to be less hazardous. In spite of these precautions, all of the spacecraft were hit by some wreckage while coasting on a sloping trajectory toward their objective. Tiny, jagged shards of metal and plastic, traveling at very high speeds, pelted the composite skin of each vehicle's wings and fuselage, leaving small craters where they impacted. The cumulative effects of the individual strikes degraded the stealth characteristics of each spaceplane in different ways, rendering all of them just a little bit more visible to military radars and other detection systems. The result was expected by engineers, pilots, and war planners, who believed the advantage of surprise outweighed the risk of damage.

* * *

Jim strolled down a dimly lit hallway, past portraits of noteworthy donors and company executives. His footfalls were muffled by dense carpet. He didn't slow down, shouldering through a pair of unlocked double doors into a well-appointed conference room.

The overhead lighting was modest. A long table, flanked by a dozen high-backed chairs, dominated the meeting space. Large tinted windows offered a panoramic view of the snow-covered city. Glare from street lights and store signs reflected off nearby building surfaces and windows, filling the night sky with an orange-white glow. Birch carvings of Alaskan animals hung on three walls, softening the atmosphere.

Ernest Marco, his expression neutral, watched Cook enter from where he sat at the far end of the conference table.

"Where's Laura Andrewyuk?" the administrator asked while quickly taking a seat near Marco.

"Change in leadership," the Hispanic shareholder replied nonchalantly. "Actually, I'm glad you're here."

"So am I."

Marco folded his hands and sat up straight. "Why are you here so late?"

"Missed my flight."

"I see." The investor nodded. "Just as well. Gives us a chance to talk face to face."

Jim leaned back in his chair. "So it would seem."

Ernest grinned. He pointed over his shoulder. "In the next room, we have a special guest. A representative. He's already met with the Board."

The starport boss glanced at the door behind Marco. "Let me guess," he suggested while making a grand gesture intended to convey mystery. "Chinese government. Unofficial. Generous offer."

"How convenient," Marco indicated while trying to get comfortable.

"You seem a little nervous," Jim observed. "Squirming around. Hands all over the place. What's on your mind?"

"Tired. Long day. You know how it is.'

Cook reached out with one hand to touch a tabletop control panel. Television screens around the room came to life with images from a statewide 24-hour news channel. The anchorman for the segment was enthusiastically reading from the teleprompter.

"We are reacting to the news of an apparent air crash just minutes ago," he related. "Sources monitoring commercial aviation radio frequencies reported a distress call coming from the executive air transport carrying Kodiak Starport Administrator James Cook. Coast Guard helicopters from Sitka and Kodiak Island are on their way to help."

Jim turned off all the televisions at once with a swipe of his finger over the control surface. "I like a good coincidence just as much as anyone else," he scolded, sitting back in his chair. "Holiday surprises are at the top of my list, too."

Ernest blushed. "You don't think we had anything to do with that?"

"Of course not," Cook turned in his chair. "I'm under contract. I can be fired. Why would you go to all that trouble…unless you needed my approval for something I might otherwise object to. You don't need my cooperation. Do you, Ernie?"

Marco bowed his head. "Very well, Mr. Cook. Let's put our cards on the table."

"Let's do that."

The suave man repositioned himself. "I know what you think of my bloc of shareholders. Our goals haven't always been in line with yours."

"That would be an understatement."

"Times change," Ernest insisted without breaking eye contact. "Nations rise and fall. Governments come and go. Corporations stand the test of time for just one reason."

"Profit and loss," Jim sighed while thumping the armrest of his chair with a fist. "Would you please cut to the chase? I'd rather die in a plane crash than hear one more minute of this!"

The door on the far side of the conference room, behind Marco, opened. A trio of nondescript men of Asian extraction entered. All three were dressed in identical tailored suits.

"Henry Cho," Jim realized when he saw the first person through the door. "Ernie? Is this the man who made an offer to the Board?"

"It is," Marco admitted while standing to greet his guest. "These are Mr. Cho's unimportant associates. Please ignore them."

Cook slid out of his chair. He stood behind it. "Marco, that man is—"

"I know who he is," Ernest huffed. "I'm aware of *what* he is, too."

Jim brushed nervously at his coat sleeve. "Henry is an ace problem solver. Hong Kong, Thailand, Singapore, and more recently the Philippines. Do I have you to thank for tonight's damage? Or was that another department's doing?"

"I may have had some small input," Cho preened in fluent English.

"You know each other?" Marco deduced.

"Heard about him," Cook continued furiously, "Ernie, this guy is—"

Henry protested mildly. "Please. There's no need for that," he assured Jim as he moved closer. "Let's you and I come to terms so that this can end well. Shall we?"

The administrator stared at Marco. "What have you agreed to?"

The enemy agent raised an index finger to get his adversary's attention. "Please direct your questions to me. It'll be quicker that way."

Jim suspected that Cho's bodyguards were armed. Even if they weren't, he wouldn't be capable of getting past both of them. They'd be highly skilled at hand-to-hand combat, and more than capable of hurting or killing him if he ran for the door or tried to make any phone calls.

"It's 11:25," Marco announced.

"I'm aware of the time," Cho rebuked without looking at the Board president. "Mr. Cook is obligated to point out that I'm a foreign government spy, just in case that might matter to you."

Jim held on to the seatback in front of him with both hands. "Ernie, this is the kind of guy who can't go home if he screws up."

"What does that mean?" Marco blinked.

"Go ahead and tell him," Henry urged as his bodyguards moved around.

The starport supervisor felt his mouth go dry. "He's got to get a specific result, or else. They'll kill people he cares about if he doesn't deliver."

"Doesn't matter," Ernest blustered. "All you have to do is order the starport to cease operation. Two years. In return, they stop their attacks for the same timeframe."

"That *is* generous."

Cho responded sympathetically. "I listened to your speech this evening. Didn't see it because I was busy with other things, but I heard every word of it. Like you, we are mindful of the future."

Cook folded his arms. "I've seen your carrot. What's the stick?"

Henry stroked his watch. "You've seen what happened to Tokyo?"

"I have."

The agent rapped his knuckles on the table. "No two starports are the same. Some are better protected than others. Even so, they're all defenseless in some way. Wouldn't you agree?"

"Please," Marco interjected. "Jim! You just said these terms are good. Why not work with us? If it's a question of compensation, I'm sure we can make arrangements. All of you! You and your whole management team. Everyone who was affected by what happened this evening!"

Cook leaned on his chair. "He knew?"

"Yes," Cho revealed. "They all did. Nobody thought you were worth saving. Consensus opinion was that the company would be better off without you."

Jim's attention fell on Marco. "He's not stretching the truth very much, is he?"

"You have always been your job," Ernest replied apologetically, "We—I admire such dedication, but it does come at a price."

"Prove it."

Henry watched Marco begin to sweat. "This isn't necessary," he implored while taking a step closer. "You're asking me to be difficult when I don't have to be. Please. While there is still time. These are good terms and we both know it."

"Convince me," the administrator demanded angrily.

Cho shrugged and took a wireless phone from his coat pocket. He showed the small screen to Cook. It displayed a digital timer with eight minutes remaining on a clock that was counting down to zero.

"Accept our offer," he said tersely while his bodyguards remained alert. "Leave the rest to a new generation of leaders. Some of the insurance policies that will rebuild your facilities are financed by banks in my country. I assure you, they will pay if you cooperate. Your vision of the future can outlive all of us."

"He's right," Marco interrupted smoothly. "It's not going to make all of our losses whole, but you get the idea. Just enough to ride out a two year slump, if they leave us alone. That's what your own report says it will take to restore basic launch services."

Jim studied Henry's expression and mannerisms for any hint of reservation that would suggest bluff or doubt. There was none as the timer on Cho's phone made a simulated ticking sound.

"What happens at 11:30?"

"This building and everyone in it will be destroyed," the Asian man admitted.

"Say that again?" Marco flinched.

Jim turned his chair so it swiveled in place. "You heard the man," he scoffed while stepping away from his rotating chair. "How many members of the Board are overnighting downstairs? Never mind. Doesn't matter. The bottom line is, Mr. Cho has leverage and I have no choice but to react."

"Just so," Henry affirmed.

The starport boss thought about his next move for two full heartbeats. He needed to present the appearance of being persuaded. "Dead men tell no tales," he pitched hesitantly. "I've been the victim of one tragedy this evening. I'd like to avoid falling prey to another."

"Understandable," Marco and Cho said at the same time.

"Let me see if I get this straight," Cook dissembled in an effort to learn more about the plot, "We cease operations for two years. That's it? No strings?"

"None," Henry assured, "Other than what it's already going to cost you and those most loyal to you. I'm told that retirement is actually quite nice. Something to be enjoyed, if one is so fortunate."

Jim's gaze deliberately went to the timer that was meant to influence him. "Just a tick less than six minutes. I assume you can stop this, if you want to?"

Cho made a slight gesture. "You know why I would have to let this happen, so let's just get this over with. We've all got better things to do."

"I've seen that tell in poker games," Cook told Marco plainly. "He's lying."

"Jim, please…" Ernest pled with a lump in his throat.

"You got me," Cook surrendered, raising both hands in the air. "Everybody that was slated to be on my bird. Quadruple our severance. You can make the air crash stick."

Henry turned to Marco. "Too much," he counseled. "Triple would be fair."

"Double," Marco bartered, "No stocks or medical. All cash, so that the expense is never made public."

"He's right," Jim confessed. "We'll take it."

"I admire your nerve," Cho laughed.

"Had to try," Cook grimaced.

Henry went to the table and reached for his phone. "Make it happen," he insisted while grasping his phone. "I'll deactivate the charges when I'm satisfied."

"Of course," Jim consented coldly. "I'd like to use the intercom. My guards. Need them to bring the encrypted phone so I can call operations at the starport."

"We have that," Marco recommended with nervous relief, "You can do it from here."

The unhappy executive stopped his moving chair. "You want total stand-down in six minutes? There's only one way I can send all the codes fast enough."

Henry's irritation increased. "Be patient, Mr. Marco. This is necessary."

Jim leaned over the table. "Tell me one thing," he wondered out loud. "What was your backup plan?"

Cho clasped both hands over his phone and held it close before putting it away.

"I see."

"What does that mean?" Marco asked.

"Squeeze play," Jim clarified.

Ernest smiled uneasily. "It won't come to that."

Cook paused with his hand on the intercom. "Always comes to that! Doesn't it, Henry?"

"Not this time," Cho insisted. "There's too much at stake. You said it yourself. Our future hangs in the balance. I regret your Board's decision, though I do approve of yours. Anyone else might have resisted. For once, my services won't be needed. I'd like to thank you for that."

Jim pressed the intercom control. "Kelly, come to the conference room right now. Bring me the big phone. I need to call home."

CHAPTER FIVE

The apparent death of a second starport administrator within just a few hours dominated international headlines. News and entertainment organizations around the world began to mention the passing of Kodiak's senior executive in sensational terms that spiked ratings.

"Tokyo's senior staff wiped out. Now this."

"The Alaskan aviation environment is unforgiving."

"Accident or mechanical failure? Stay tuned for more details!"

A preliminary statement from the Kodiak Starport's media relations division merely explained that, "All available resources are being directed to the crisis. More information will be forthcoming when rescuers on the scene can report something specific."

* * *

Kelly approached the secretary's desk incredulously. "Say that again?"

"Bring the big phone," Jim told her, speaking precisely. "I don't like the situation here."

"On our way."

"Just you," he demanded. "The others can go."

"Be with you in a minute."

She turned away from the silent man behind the small desk and walked to the middle of the lobby, where she whispered to her expectant subordinates. "Looks like this *is* something," she told them quietly.

"How do you want to play it?" one man asked.

The team leader avoided any physical movement. "Last guy to have my job didn't go far enough. That's why I got promoted. So. Let's assume the worst. Get downstairs. No radios. Wait for my signal. Three-way play."

The other man on her left nodded. "Team One preps for evac," he suggested.

His colleague scratched an exposed wrist. "Team Two handles extraction."

Haines remained soft-spoken. "Sounds good. Do it. Team three dismounts the convoy. Have them prep for counterassault. Do nothing if you hear nothing. Go if you get my signal."

"What's that going to be?" one of them wanted to know.

"Anything that isn't 'all clear,'" she decided.

* * *

Conditions inside the starport's recently renovated air defense bunker were tense. Norman Ahgupuk struggled to maintain his composure while traffic coordinators continued to manage search and rescue operations with Coast Guard officials who were dispatching helicopters from Kodiak and Sitka air stations.

Knowing the truth—that Cook's crash wasn't real—didn't make his task any easier.

"Crash plus 30," a stopwatch-wielding man shouted.

"That's it," Norman confirmed, "Nobody survives winter water for more than 20 minutes, even with survival gear."

A phone receiver on his console chirped for attention. He answered after the first beep. "Administrator Two," Raven said, identifying herself formally. "I've got a count of 30 minutes. You know what that means?"

"Yes, ma'am, I do," the pilot replied while making a note in his log with a ballpoint pen. "I don't like the timing of this incident."

"What's your recommendation?"

Norman appeared to stop and think. "I sent up the alert fighters when we got the distress call," he said, enunciating clearly for the benefit of his audience. "I'd like them to stretch their legs. Keep 'em up there for a while so my pilots can get some hours."

"No objections," Raven decided.

"I'd like to expand our combat patrol radius," he added as he scanned the nearby navigation displays.

"Why?" Frost questioned for the benefit anyone who might be eavesdropping.

Norman wrote more notes in his log. "The nature of this crash indicates sabotage," he declared. "I want to put gatekeeper on high guard for the next ten days, just to be safe. Call it a training exercise when the media asks."

"Nobody will believe that so close to Christmas," Raven pretended to object.

Ahgupuk became adamant. "Nobody from this office will talk. Even so, the facts will come out. Always do. That means—"

"I know," Raven relented, "You've got my full support. Make it happen."

Ahgupuk hung up. He turned to face the nearest group of section leaders. "What did you see and when did you see it? Data and transcripts to me in 15 minutes! Assign field inspectors. Crash analysis begins at first light."

* * *

Beatrice Brown frowned at the phone in her hand as she walked in to the starport's busy television studio wearing a phthalo blue jacket. "Where is he, if he's not actually dead?"

"We're making this up as we go along."

The head of the company's recently created news division stepped aside to let two technicians go by.

"That's just great!" she huffed, "I'm supposed to read the copy and cry for the camera?"

"Our lies are your lies."

"Please don't quote Jim to me," Beatrice griped.

"Truth hurts," Frost kidded. "Lawyers are on their way to advise you. Stick to the crash theme until they get there. Hoopla and speculation. Sinking wreckage. Not much to see in the dark. Hard to recover in rough seas. That sort of thing. We'll find a subject matter expert for you to chat with."

* * *

Henry Cho whispered with the guards while Jim waited. "You'll be happy to know that your staff is acting competently," he commented as he stepped around the conference table. "Doing just what they should, now that you've made your displeasure known."

"You can't expect me to let you kill all these people," Jim frowned.

"Of course not," Henry conceded as one of his guards opened a door to admit Kelly Haines. She walked in slowly, holding the communications case in one hand. The muscular man made momentary eye contact with her as he shut the door.

Haines walked away from him, around the table, to stand near Cook. She laid the aluminum case on the table and shuffled back two steps to improve her view of the entire area.

"Please tell her to go," Marco requested solicitously from his position at the far end of the long table.

"Couldn't if I wanted to," Cook lied, "She signed for this and it's very expensive. I'm still on the hook for a few pieces of office equipment I can't find, and—"

"Yes," Cho interrupted abruptly, "I'm familiar with the problem."

"They put you through this, too?"

Henry stroked his wrist, as if tapping an imaginary timepiece. "Yes. Now, if you would, please, get on with it."

"Jim? That's a real thing?" Ernest questioned shyly.

Cook flopped into his chair and reached for the communications carrier. "You'd know things like this if you really worked for a living," he complained to the venture capitalist while opening the case with his thumb print. "Hm. Let me see. Been a while. I think..."

"Are you a qualified communications technician?" Henry asked Kelly. "We are somewhat pressed for time. Can you help Mr. Cook?"

"No, sir," she fudged. "I just carry the box."

Cho regarded Jim skeptically.

The starport executive glared back at him. "Don't tread on me, Henry. I might start to think you're not a man of your word."

"What would make you say that?" Marco inquired furtively.

"The fact that he's still here," Cook observed while opening the case with this thumbprint. Indicator lights winked on as touch screens came to life. "In addition to many other talents, Henry has a knack for being somewhere else when his bombs go off."

Ernest turned from left to right in an effort to suggest that he was still in control. "I see no reason why you should be so paranoid."

Jim typed an access code using the only visible keypad in the case, while touching an empty corner of the instrument panel as if he were pressing a button. He picked up one of two handsets from the console and looked directly at Henry.

"How's your family?"

Cho's expression went blank. "That's really not an appropriate question."

Cook's heart sank with the implied loss behind that rebuke, causing him to be speechless. "Yeah," he said up after a lurching breath. "I'm just not ready for this."

Henry sensed something amiss as Kelly reacted. She'd seen Jim pick up the wrong handset. Hearing him say a prearranged phrase was the last clue that she was being prompted to take action.

"Please don't do anything foolish," Cho told her as Jim's phone chirped through its dialing sequence.

"I'm not paid to think." She smiled with one hand on a pad clipped to her vest. Moving two fingers casually over the smooth face of the black wireless device, she pressed a pair of raised keys that caused her digital radio to send a short transmission.

* * *

The brief monotone pulse was an ordinary test signal, commonly used by technicians to determine strength and reception clarity. Acting on verbal instructions passed to them minutes earlier, units in various locations throughout the building reacted to the long beep sounding through their squad net.

Members of Team One began working their way through the tenth floor executive quarters, knocking on doors. They whispered softly to each person who greeted them. Team Two boarded an elevator in the underground parking garage. Team Three left half their strength with the six-vehicle convoy. They jogged in single file up three flights of stairs to the ground level.

* * *

Uniformed men and women in charge of building security, employed by a local civilian contractor, watched the subtle evacuation unfold from the comfort of a locked command post on the fifth floor.

"Where do you suppose they're going at this hour?" somebody asked.

"Armed and armored," an observant man gestured with his coffee mug, "Action in the garage. They're going through barriers like they aren't even there."

"That means they have passcodes," a voice ventured.

"Wait," the shift supervisor urged as he read from a large flat panel. "The manual says to call for guidance. Buzz the lobby and tell 'em what's happening. Alert the patrols." He fumed, reaching for a phone, "Protocol doesn't say exactly who I should bother for something like this. Give me a minute to work it out."

* * *

Raven Frost was sitting on the administrator's dais in the middle of the main operations area, surrounded by technicians with handheld computers, when Jim's call came in. "I wasn't expecting to hear from you," she yawned. "We're still spinning the crash. Lots to coordinate. What can I do for you?"

Cook sat back in his chair. The corporate conference room became suddenly quiet as he pressed a button on the console that put the conversation on speaker. "Sorry to bother you with anything at a time like this." He laid the receiver down, turning the console in Henry's direction so that even Marco could see the starport's transmission. "I have an important matter to discuss. It can't wait."

The deputy administrator's face filled the screen. "What's this all about?"

"Please listen very carefully." Jim raised his voice. "I'm going to give you a direct order. I want you to follow it. Do you understand?"

"Yes," Raven replied slowly, looking at Henry Cho with new interest.

"You see this fella next to Marco? Do you know who he is?" he probed.

"I think so."

"You know what that means?" he hinted.

"Yes," she confirmed without hesitation.

Henry cast a disapproving look at Jim. The administrator grinned apologetically. "They've got me over a barrel. That's why I want you to do exactly what I'm about to tell you. No argument. Are we clear?"

"I understand." Raven nodded while gesturing off camera.

Jim took a deep breath. "It's not all Henry's handiwork," he explained. "The Board gave in. Tonight's aerial extravaganza was meant to seal the deal. I need to ask you for something hard."

"I'm ready."

"Apple cart," Cook stated succinctly.

Readouts inside the communications carrier winked out as the device turned off.

* * *

"What did you do?" Henry demanded.

"Shoot 'em," Jim told Kelly.

Pulling her pistol, Haines fired on Cho's bodyguards. Both of them collapsed to the carpet with gaping head wounds. The sudden report of gunshots startled Ernest Marco, who dove under the conference table as a phone began to buzz.

"Don't even think about it," Cook told Henry.

"Hands up!" Kelly shouted while taking a step forward the startled man.

"Yes!" Henry choked while showing his palms.

The phone rang again. Jim reached over the table to turn it off.

"This is inexcusable!" Ernest blustered as he got to his feet.

The irate starport boss shook his head while pointing at the apprehensive agent, "*You* are inexcusable! You agreed to let him kill me, then you gave him the go-ahead to blow up this building!"

"There is still time to get out!" Marco exclaimed.

"We are certainly going to try."

"Two minutes," Cho muttered.

Jim tugged on his suit coat. "Nice try. I've been briefed on how you operate. There's a minder next door who is here to make sure this job gets done. They won't care if we make a run for it, so long as the charges you placed go off on time."

Footfalls in the hallway, punctuated by sounds of surprise and protest from the foyer guard, announced the arrival of the executive retrieval team. The conference room quickly filled with armed guards.

"Rear guard! Shoot anyone who comes through that door," Kelly pointed.

"Nicely done," Cook said approvingly as he rushed for the open hallway.

"What about him?" somebody asked.

Ernest held on to the back of his chair in fearful silence as Kelly nudged her prisoner into motion.

"Mr. Marco can find his own way out!"

Chapter Six

Alarms sounded across the Kodiak Starport. Emergency service vehicles roared through the darkness, down access roads leading to important installations. Armed security personnel rushed to stations in sensitive areas.

Activity in the underground operations center reached fever pitch as technicians scrambled to make marginal systems work. Raven Frost stood on the raised platform behind the administrator's high-backed chair to get a better look at the chaos. Her wireless headset crackled with chatter that reflected the tension.

She leaned over her chair to read off the next item as it came up on her checklist display. "All departments, all stations, confirm follow-through on published lockdown procedures in 60 seconds. Confirm special measures for media and execute. I don't want Foss or Brown complaining about resources!"

Voices in her ear signaled their understanding as supervisors continued to act. Raven touched a screen to give her approval as text messages materialized. "Open channel," she told her device.

"Select," it prompted in a synthetic voice.

"Air defense," she ordered. Computer-driven systems reacted to her voice, transmitting the order to Norman Ahgupuk's location. He responded a second later. "On line. Reset complete. Data links are coming up now. Clear skies. Gatekeeper is rolling."

Frost was about to turn her attention to another matter when a news item on a nearby television caught her attention. "You seeing this?" she asked Norman. Voices around the cavernous chamber hushed as attention focused on what local reporters were saying.

"—explosions wrecked the upper floors of Shadow Fusion Enterprises just moments ago. As you can see, the entire building is on fire. It's coming down in large parts, filling the surrounding area with flaming debris."

"Was he in there?"

The deputy glanced at her desk. "Hotline remains quiet. Orders are still in effect."

"That's not the kind of thing you take back," the retired officer reflected without taking his eyes off the unfolding carnage. "What a mess. I'm going upstairs. Hang around for a while. See what I see."

"It's late," she objected. "Don't go. Let your expensive pilots handle it."

Norman chuckled. "I'll be down and done before your head finds a pillow."

Raven struggled with an inner conflict while she read the rapidly scrolling reports that appeared and vanished on her displays. "What makes you think I sleep?"

"See all, know all?" Ahgupuk jested.

"Yes," she sniffed.

"What happens if—"

Raven cleared her throat. "Yes. Somebody will get around to promoting me, and then I'll be your boss. Somebody else gets my job and all of us get to live with it. Now, please, go. I'd prefer it if you went home. We've got a crisis to manage."

* * *

International response to the implosion of a starport's corporate headquarters was mixed to the point of being understated because the event hadn't actually taken place at a space launch facility. Commentators took sober note of the rising death toll from the comfort of their studios as police and fire units converged on the worsening scene.

"—still not sure who got out," a contracted security specialist explained when asked by a diligent local news reporter. "Not even sure what it was all about. Alarms went off and we started asking people to leave. That's what they pay us for, so that's what we did."

The excited journalist checked the position of his camera. "We've got an unconfirmed sighting of Starport Administrator Cook; that he was seen here, in the building. Can you shed any light on that?"

A uniformed security contractor who had just escaped from the collapsing structure shook his head as snow fell around him. "No, sir. Couldn't if I wanted to. Company policy. We don't comment on the whereabouts of customers or their employees."

The garrulous reporter turned away from his subject, so that the field of view as seen by his digital camera would change. "You heard it here first. Police and fire are still arriving. More details when they become available. Now, back to the studio for an update on other stories we're following at this hour, including sports and weather."

* * *

Raven's heart raced. She sat in her chair while thinking about the task at hand, rather than how friends and colleagues perished under tons of burning wreckage. "Emergency lockout complete in 20 seconds!" somebody called out.

With one eye on the activity around her, the former engineer watched new data spill onto the screens in front of her. Every command and administrative clearance granted to Jim Cook and the members of his travelling staff would be revoked within a matter of seconds. None of them would be capable of issuing any order through company channels, assuming they were still alive.

Jim's death and the decapitation of the company's Board of Directors suggested dire consequences for the starport. The appearance of a known provocateur like Henry Cho, just hours after the destruction of Tokyo's launch complex, indicated to Raven that the threat to the Kodiak facility was imminent.

"Open channel," she vocalized softly.

"Select," her device replied dispassionately.

"Nanook," Frost indicated while turning in her seat.

"Authenticate," the synthetic voice challenged.

"Send the wise bear," she said in her native tongue.

After a series of clicks and chirps, aerospace coordinator Raphael Chandler answered. "Good morning, Deputy. We've been looking at the mission package you sent. That's quite the tall order."

Raven reached for a tablet to look at what she'd sent him. "Complicated trajectory. Multiple targets. Yes, I can see why you might not like it."

"Not my problem," he responded after a swig of coffee. "We just put 'em on the catapults and keep the runways clean. The intelligence unit will get back to you with their complaints. I'm just here to ask for the usual."

"Begin fueling," she ordered.

"Strike or intercept?" he inquired while working his way through a series of touch screens.

"Strike."

"Targets?" Raphe asked when the next checklist popped up.

Frost looked at a map of the world on the ceiling over her workstation. "Work from the list I gave you."

"That's a lot of targets for just a few ships."

"I know that," she emphasized

"You really want to visit all those exotic places?"

"Yes!" she demanded.

"Ordnance?"

"Rod penetrators," Raven recited from memory.

"Six thousand pounds each," the A.C. informed her, "Two payloads per ship. Your shopping list doesn't leave any room for errors. Anything they miss goes unharmed."

The administrator turned to stare at a holographic projection of the Kodiak Starport. "That's a risk we have to take."

Chandler reexamined his copy of the target list on a secondary monitor. "Frankly, we're surprised that you don't want to do more damage. Targeting their underground runways is smart. I like that. Kinda sorta expecting them to dig for ours. Hitting their deep data storage is going to hurt, but it won't put Jiuquan out of action for more than a few months. I can't see them doing that here."

"Too much escalation," Frost told him directly. "I don't need the ghost of Jim Cook flying around to know that. We've got to stop this technological backslide."

"You're pulling a punch," he warned.

"I have a plan."

"So do they!" he shot back, "It's called turning us in to a pile of rocks."

"Not if we change their minds," Raven admonished, "Governments and corporations have a lot in common. They both run on complicated bureaucracies. That means they can be influenced."

"What's that supposed to mean?"

"It's all in how you ask," she laughed.

The A.C. sat motionless. "This I gotta hear."

Frost clutched a fistful of printed pages on her desk. "Deep data storage is nothing more than a pile of computers, information storage, and expensive spare parts," she lectured while dropping the paper, "It's important because we say so. We keep quiet about these locations, because they are so valuable in a crisis. What happens if we threaten theirs?"

"They feel obliged to threaten ours?" Raphe supposed. "Seems kinda silly."

Raven shook her head. "You're thinking like an engineer. They're looking at this differently."

"Politics."

She nodded. "We can always earn more money and rebuild our reputation. We can't easily replace institutional knowledge or the rockets that take us back to space. Especially the big stuff. Billion dollar systems and infrastructure have to be saved because they're gone when we lose the tools to make them."

"You are…tempting them to pull their punch?"

Frost hesitated. Her mental machinations were still coming into focus. Acting without full authority was dangerous, both to herself and everyone she supervised. "It's all in how you ask," she lied.

"So many miracles in one day," Chandler appreciated humorously, "You'll be a superstar if this works out. Your mission package is logged in. Intell should get back to you with refinements. Since we're on the subject of asking for things, Mr. Ahgupuk filed a request with the aviation armory for our ASM's. Will you release?"

"Ours are experimental," she objected.

"Sounds like no."

"I do say no," Raven decided. "What he's asking for may not work and we've only got four of them. No. I don't—won't risk using them. If we do get hit by an aerospace attack, he may kill those pilots—"

"—without those weapons!" he pled.

"Request denied."

* * *

"Facility lockdown complete!" a voice shouted behind Raven. She stood up to see 50 faces turned in her direction. The weight of every gaze in the room fell on her.

"Intercom," she instructed. The device in her ear signaled with a chime as she mounted the step behind her chair to be seen by everyone in the area. "Turn off the televisions," she insisted through the public address system. "All of them. We've had enough of that."

Voices murmured. Hands moved. Keys clicked as screens winked out around the large room. Raven forced herself to continue. "There is…" she cringed without any attempt to hide her grief. "I mean—you saw it, so there's no point in trying to deny it. It was what it looks like. I have to assume they are…gone."

Some of the technicians looked away. Others quietly swore while the deputy administrator forged ahead. "Reset command codes and change administrative protocols," she instructed gravely. "Don't think about it. Just do your job and remember what happened to Tokyo. All this trouble means we're next."

Andre Allison elbowed his way in to an open space. The launch coordinator reached for a plastic whistle around his neck and blew out a sharp tweet. "All sections, get back to work and report!"

* * *

Jet engines roared as Norman approached four pilots standing near a hangar exit. The section leaders who managed his squadron stopped talking as he came into view. They were clad in helmets and high altitude flight suits decorated with Kodiak Starport logos, rank tabs, and unit patches that attested to their past service in national air forces or private companies.

"Change of spec," the former Air Force Major told his handpicked section leaders while zipping his insulated collar closed. "Get out there and have 'em reload our birds for aerospace engagement. All other ships remain fitted as they are, for standard air-to-air combat."

"We don't have authorization for that ordnance," Harris Hancock, a former Canadian Air Force Captain, objected.

"Who said I was going to ask?" Ahgupuk scoffed.

"What do you know?" Rupert Carson, a former U.S. Air Force lieutenant, asked.

Norman went to a nearby workbench and picked up his helmet. "Nothing more than you do," he lied, "but I'm putting the pieces together. Tokyo. Company headquarters. It's not a rumor. They got Cook. Now the boss wants us to fly maximum patrol radius."

He pulled an insulated cap onto his head before putting his helmet on. Knowing about the starport's aerospace capability didn't make his job any easier. "Everything I see tells me that trouble is coming to breakfast."

The pilots laughed away their worry. "You're asking us to get in the way?" Alejandro Lopez, a former Mexican Air Force lieutenant jeered softly.

Ahgupuk reached for a pair of heavy gloves. "Not asking. Telling. Load for high altitude intercept, just like we would in the service."

"Why not reconfigure the entire flight?" Hancock proposed.

The squadron commander shook his head. "We're the only career pilots on payroll who trained extensively for this kind of thing. There's only four working weapons in stock—one for each of us. They won't give them to us, so we'll take them and hope for mercy later on, when we're heroes."

All four men looked at each other with raw skepticism, then at Norman. He spread his hands. "If anyone can make that kind of shot under stress, it would be you bunch of pirates," he suggested grandly.

"Not in my contract—but I'm in," Carson shrugged.

"Already been unemployed once," Lopez grinned.

Ahgupuk turned his attention the last holdout in their midst. "What do you say?" he coaxed. "It would mean a lot at our legal review if this was a team effort."

Connor Beck, formerly a lieutenant in the Texas Air National Guard, rolled his eyes. "Beats flyin' tourists to places I never heard of," he concluded after a long pause.

Norman beamed. "We might all be doing that if this goes wrong. So, let me tell you how this happens. Beck, you'll stay. I'm taking your place for this one."

"Fine by me," the Texan consented. "You need somebody to buffalo the ordnance chief, anyway."

"You've done that before?"

"Mebbe," Connor replied nonchalantly.

* * *

Loss of Kodiak Starport's high profile leadership rocked Alaska's aviation community. Local, national, and international media personalities who could get statements or interviews went on air as quickly as possible with responses ranging from dispassionate fact to inflamed opinion or outrageous speculation.

Beatrice Brown responded to all of it from her desk in the center of a newly remodeled soundstage, surrounded by holographic displays that only she could see from her centrally placed pivoting chair. "Anchorage police and fire units are still converging," she explained to the orbiting cameras and microphones. "You're seeing live camera feeds from several different networks and independent reporters as they try to get closer to what was the physical location of our parent company."

Electrically operated swing arms rotated silently on sweeping gimbals to move each digital device around her as the well-dressed woman continued her choreographed narration with a notepad computer in one hand. The burning skyscraper appeared to scintillate behind her as Kyle Foss gave orders to special effects technicians.

"Feed on five is too shaky. Switch to six."

A dozen upper floors of the Shadow Fusion Building collapsed in a thunderous roar, scattering tons of debris in a two-block radius. The experienced media manager looked at his wristwatch. "Have we got Richter?"

"Line two," an assistant whispered.

Foss keyed his microphone, speaking directly to Beatrice. "Your wish has been granted," he joked good-humoredly.

Beatrice smiled at the nearest camera as it passed by without pausing in her commentary. "The collapse of our corporate headquarters leaves very little doubt in anyone's mind that the loss of life has been substantial. We're still trying to get an accurate assessment from officials in the Anchorage Fire Department who can speak directly to the structural nature of what you're witnessing. In the meantime, I now have the opportunity to speak with Kodiak Starport's head of security, Mr. Billy Richter."

"Good evening Ms. Brown," Billy's voice boomed through a telephone connection, "Or should I say good morning, because it's just a little after one o'clock in the a.m.?"

"I'm sorry we don't have the luxury of talking under better circumstances," Brown said, nodding formally. "Of all the things to be trending on social media at this hour, I wish we could be talking about something else. What can you tell us about the situation so far?"

Richter sighed. "There is some good news. Our building safety detachment was on the ball. The shift supervisor noticed that something was amiss and sounded the alarm. For that reason, some, but not all, of the building's occupants got out."

"What was this?"

"We're still assessing," Billy generalized, "If you don't mind, I've got a lot on my plate just now. Give me a few more hours to—"

"Who was in there and who got out?"

Richter paused so that he would sound like he was deliberately obfuscating. "It's amazing that anyone got out at all," he breathed through the phone line. "Somebody was a hero. I'll tell you more when I know more."

* * *

Billy laid the black plastic phone down and stepped away from the administrator's desk. His uniform and boots were indistinguishable from any other starport soldier, except for rank tabs and security clearance badges that granted him access to the entire facility.

He wiped both hands on his flanks, as if they were dirty. "That's not going to keep them happy."

Raven Frost watched his every move from where she sat. "It'll keep the media off my back just long enough to get some things done."

"I can imagine," Richter chuckled.

"Can you?"

He bowed his head. "Some of it is racism," he observed candidly. "Maybe a little sexism. Until just now, you've been the Number Two."

"What was it like for you?"

Billy shuffled in place with real mirth. "Soldiers and cops are just as opinionated as anyone," he snorted. "They gave me a lot of grief."

"What did you do about it?"

"Muscled through," Billy assured. "Can I offer you some advice?"

"Sure."

He spread his hands to gesture at the spartan interior of the room they were in. "There's a reason this office is decked out like it is. You're not supposed to like it in here. It's just comfy enough to work, but just irritating enough to make you get out of that chair and go see what's happening."

"Gloomy."

Richter took a step back. "Jim's dead. I don't need to be in Anchorage to know that. It'll take weeks to find whatever is left of him and the folks who were with him. I'm sure their families will be grateful. Right or wrong, good or bad, this is your best chance to show everyone who works here that you're worthy of being called Number One."

Raven sat up. "I know the dangers of indecision."

Billy was insistent. "I've seen two different styles of management from the men who filled that chair. One was hands-on. The other delegated whenever he could. They were both out and about, all the time. Never in this room more than they had to be. That's my advice. Don't be in here anymore than you've just got to be."

Frost got to her feet. "I've been thinking about that. The paperwork that promotes me to senior administrator should be coming through any time now. When that happens, I'll be bound to do some things by the book, if you know what I mean."

Richter looked at a cabinet on the far wall that contained an encrypted executive printer. "Let's pretend that I do," he suggested glibly.

She walked around the desk. "Tell me about The Bloody Bucket," she whispered.

"I don't know what you're talking about."

"Of course not," she conceded tactfully. "I understand your concern. Anything you and I talk about before I'm officially promoted should be remembered as hypothetical. There's no reason you should be held accountable for what might come of this."

"You have something in mind?"

"I do."

The tall man lowered his voice. "It would mean my job if the *Deputy* Administrator gets caught."

"I know what I'm asking for."

"Give me the short version that keeps me out of jail," he demanded.

The persistent woman looked him in the eye. "If the analysts are right, we're about to be hit by an aerospace attack. All I want to do is stack the deck in our favor."

"How?"

"Misdirection," Raven responded forcefully.

He wasn't impressed. "You're asking for a sit-down with the most hardened criminals this side of the Arctic Circle without the full weight and authority of a position you don't have yet. How are you going to fake them, and how does that work for us?"

"By asking them for something we would want in a crisis like this," Raven hinted. "A location. Someplace very specific inside Jiuquan starport that can only be damaged by ground penetrating weapons."

The former soldier's eyebrows rose, then lowered, with sudden understanding. "Naturally, our friends at The Bloody Bucket will sell us out. One of them will, even if their leadership promised otherwise. I like it."

"There's more to it—"

"Don't tell me," he interrupted. "I really do want to know, but I shouldn't…just in case you have to testify in front of Congress. One of us needs to be clean."

"Covering all the bases," she sighed.

"It's all about stopping problems before they start," he laughed. "What happens if the attack we've planned for doesn't come tonight?"

Frost laid a hand on her desk. "Hours, days, or weeks. Doesn't matter. They didn't just inconvenience Tokyo. They destroyed it. There won't be any space launch from that real estate ever again. That means whatever is in the works for us happens tonight."

"We'll slip out of here while everyone is still trying to cope with the change in leadership," Richter recommended. "It'll be a short meeting. Won't take more than a half an hour."

"Great!"

"This isn't your usual business meeting," he stipulated. "There are rules to this that can't be broken. I'll explain them to you as we go. Look for a change of wardrobe down the hall, in a room with no numbers on the door. I'm not supposed to give you the key until you've actually been—never mind! Leave your phone, radio, and all forms of executive identification in the concealed compartment under your chair."

Raven leaned over to inspect the carpet. "Where is it? I had no idea."

"Welcome to your new life!"

Chapter Seven

Governor Wheeler's chartered passenger jet was still in flight when he was urgently requested by his chief of staff to redirect. "We've stirred the pot with rumors connected to Cook's death," his longtime friend and adviser told him. "Everybody with a briefcase is leaving town. State Troopers are locking the doors and turning off the lights. It'll take a week to go through this town thoroughly enough satisfy the right people that it's okay to come back. Hopefully, that's enough for Kodiak to get a handle on their situation."

"Did they really kill him?" Wheeler wondered, eyeing a small television screen.

"Don't go there," his handler insisted. "Just give us a few days to sort things. Go to Fairbanks. Say something to the press when you land. Respectful. Grief. That sort of thing. It'll be something like 2 a.m. when you get there, so the only person you might chat with will be that guy from the Daily News Miner."

The politician glanced at a clock. "I can't—"

"You should!" his consultant interrupted. "Sheldon, this is war. I'm just glad it wasn't you. We've put a lot of money in to that starport. Let 'em earn it."

Wheeler shivered when he heard the oblique reference to Nanook. He laid down the beige handset to break the connection without saying another word and waved to get the attention of his aid. "Tell the pilot to turn around. Take us to Fairbanks."

"Would you like me to wake your wife?"

"No," Sheldon stiffened. "It's going to be a long night. One of us may as well pass the time without anything to worry about."

* * *

Raven got off the subterranean monorail dressed in stained cold weather gear. Her hair was pulled back in a bun, hidden beneath a black stocking cap. Her insulated work boots clunked on the platform as she shuffled through garbage and snow to blend in with a throng of men and women who left the station in a noisy gaggle.

Cold air blasted through the subway tunnel as another train arrived. The disguised executive followed Billy's instructions to the letter, going up the escalator to the surface without making eye contact with anyone. Some of the gregarious men and women were out shopping. Others were getting off work. Tobacco haze filled the air as a brazen few ignored the obvious 'No Smoking' signs.

Raven stayed away from anyone wearing red or green jumpsuits. Fuelers and coolant loaders were notorious for thinking poorly of starport management, whom they often ridiculed on sight. Because time was a factor, she was forced to walk through the worst of the employee housing block to reach the entertainment zone, which most people called "Boom Town."

Frost recalled that visitors and staff alike sometimes joked about how everyone and everything in that part of the starport was for sale, if you knew who to ask and how to pay. She tried not to think about that criminal factoid while making her way through a series of covered walkways over a distance of nine city blocks before reaching her destination.

The Bloody Bucket was one of the oldest bars and hangouts for hustlers inside the starport's official perimeter. Loud music bellowed from speakers mounted high on the interior walls of what had once been a warehouse. Pulsating bass notes rattled the wrinkled sheet metal on the outside of the old structure in time with the prerecorded music.

Raven paid the cover charge at the door and let the aging bouncer frisk her while handing over a fake I.D. for his inspection.

"What's your business here?" the big man requested civilly while returning her credentials.

Even with hand-me-down clothes, Frost didn't fit the profile of a bar hopper in the bad part of town and she knew it. "I know the owner," she told him as per script.

The enforcer grunted and moved on to the next patron when he heard the code phrase. Raven made her way across the crowded dance floor to the bar. She paused to look for a foot rail before putting one boot on a rusty rail and taking off her hat. A bald bartender approached with a puzzled look on his face.

"May I help you?"

Raven looked over her shoulder. "You're not wrong," she told him with a smile meant to be reassuring. "I am Ms. Smith."

The bartender looked down at a touch screen display that only he could see. Starport administrators had started the sign and counter-sign decades ago. "You must be the new guy," he decided after reading a few lines of text.

"Yes," Frost nodded with her hat in both hands. "I'm the new guy."

The wary man grimaced and poured a draft of foaming cold beer from a nearby tap. "Have yourself a drink on the house," he invited, sliding the cool glass to a stop in front of Raven. "Give me a minute to take care of some things."

The worried woman took the glass as it was offered, knowing that this, too, was another part of the countersign process, to ensure that she was alone and acting of her own accord. She drank slowly before raising her voice to be heard over the crowd. "Thank you," she called while forcing down cheap beer.

"You're welcome," her host shouted.

He reached under the bar to push a button. "Finish your drink, then go on back. The folks need a minute to get presentable."

Frost regarded the suds in her mug with mixed feelings before chugging them down. She recalled Billy's long list of dos and don'ts, which had included following the bartender's instructions, no matter how strange they might seem.

"Not what you're used to?"

"No," she confessed while wiping her chin with a stained sleeve.

The bartender winked. "Tell you what…Deputy. I'll see what I can do about that, if you'll come visit us a little more often. Sound fair?"

Frost remained in outward control of her expression as her heart skipped a beat. Before going their separate ways, Billy had warned her that some of the people she'd meet would know surprisingly intimate details about her. This man was obviously one of the better informed residents of Boom Town. "Any advice for a first timer?" she wisecracked to hide her uneasiness.

"Don't give without getting," he advised while pointing to a door labeled 'Employees Only.'

"Wouldn't do anything else," Raven reached over the bar to put five dollars in the man's tip jar.

"Don't do that," he blushed.

"You probably own this place," she joked. "Even I know good advice when I hear it."

The apprehensive executive went to the end of the bar, stuffing her hat into a deep cargo pocket. A tall, muscular man stood by himself near the employee's entrance watching her approach. The guard held a studded metal door open, allowing her to enter without comment. Raven was greeted by another athletic sentry sitting on a stool just inside a short dimly lit hallway.

"What's the word?" he questioned without moving from his perch.

"Halftime," Frost replied as instructed by Billy, who had briefed her on every detail necessary to enter the inner sanctum of the starport's larcenous underworld.

"They're expecting you," the bouncer replied, gesturing at a door at the end of the corridor.

"I'm sure they are."

Hearing about this criminal syndicate behind closed doors was one thing. Coming face-to-face with it would be something else. Reinforced walls shielded by dense anti-surveillance electronics protected the spacious room. Its tasteful interior was decorated with expensive furniture. A full-service bar flanked by wall-mounted displays dominated half the visible space.

Raven reminded herself that this lavish lair was inhabited by members of the most ruthless association of criminals on starport soil. All other gangs and crews that snuck or stole inside the launch complex were weak by comparison. Her eyes adjusted to reduced illumination as predatory heads turned to assess her with the briefest of practiced glances.

A dozen men and women whom she knew very little about sat around a large circular table. Frost smiled at them individually as she took the only empty seat at the table. "Good evening," she hailed while sitting. "Thank you for seeing me on such short notice."

Her greeting was met by noncommittal noises from those present. Anthony Siggs got to his feet. The middle-aged businessman smoothed his suit coat with one hand. "Good evening, Mrs. Frost," he began politely. "I am truly sorry for your losses. It's a pity that we've got to meet under these conditions."

Raven shook the hand he offered with a firm grip. "Thanks very much. I knew you'd understand."

The merciless merchant who'd sell anything for the right price released her hand and withdrew to his chair with a nod to the woman seated on the other side of him. "I told you she'd be here sooner than later," he preened.

Wanda Ness eyed Raven while texting with a wireless phone in each hand. Her ebony features remained placid. "Interesting that a deputy administrator comes to call so soon after all that trouble," the convicted accountant observed. "I didn't think they'd let you off the chain so soon."

"That chain works both ways."

Siggs and Ness looked at each other. Raven remained quiet as the gathered men and women whispered about her. The starport's criminal cartel wasn't that much different than any other business. Profit and loss mattered. Everyone with a seat at this table was a member of a very corrupt Board of Directors, bent on success at any price.

Siggs was the cartel's current board president because he controlled the largest number of shares, which meant he could bankroll their most profitable ventures. Wanda was their version of a senior administrator because she commanded enough loyalty from lesser factions to get most things done, within acceptable losses.

An expensive, handcrafted, birch chair moved easily on casters when Raven tried to get comfortable. She made her own assessment of the people seated around the table. Years of corporate intrigues and professional setbacks prepared her for this moment. "My husband keeps telling me I should hang out with a better class of people."

Several of the female observers laughed.

"Explains why we didn't see a ring on your finger," Wanda kidded mildly.

Frost shrugged. "Don't see one on yours."

"Same reason you don't wear yours," Ness conceded.

The pro tem starport boss sat forward to project greater authority. "I wish we had time to be social, but I've got a crisis on my hands. This thing with China is getting out of hand."

"Hard to miss," Siggs empathized.

"They *didn't* miss." Raven rapped her bare knuckles on the tabletop. "My boss is dead. That forces me to respond. In your own way, I'm sure you can understand my position. Yes?"

"Blood for blood," Wanda agreed.

"This isn't one of your gang wars," Frost shook her head. "I can't just hurt 'em back and hope they go away. Escalation is out of the question."

"Don't mess with what works!" somebody jeered.

Raven sat back and spread her hands. "None of this works anymore if we keep tearing each other apart. Stop it now, or we're out of business. That means more than poverty for you. It's the end of spaceflight for all of us—and the start of something we may not be able to stop."

"Go on," Siggs motioned.

The administrator looked around the table, making eye contact with each person as she spoke. "I need to force a stop to the fighting, so that all surviving starports retain their capabilities. We need to keep what we've got left or risk losing it altogether. Follow me?"

"An interesting proposition," the cartel's leader accepted when a majority nodded or leaned in with gestures of approval. "We're not engineers or politicians, so the finer points of what you're suggesting don't seem obvious. What's our part in this?"

"I want the most up-to-date layout of the Jiuquan starport," Raven explained. "More specifically, I want to know where their deep data storage is."

"The first part is no problem," Anthony affirmed with an overly sweet smile. "What makes you think we'd know—"

"You know where ours is…"

"I'm sure we don't," he insisted. "Even if we did, that's one detail we'd never—"

Raven turned her attention to Wanda. "The only reason you haven't is because they haven't asked. Or am I wrong?"

"They wouldn't meet our price," Ness admitted with a grin while putting her phones aside.

The revelation made Frost angry. "Anthony. Please. Have what I'm asking for on my desk by the time I get back to my office, or I'll—"

"That's not the arrangement we have!"

Raven kept her attention focused on Wanda, as if Siggs didn't matter. "I'm not the senior administrator just yet. Paperwork hasn't come through. Any decisions I make right now are all mine, as the Number Two."

"What are you saying?" Anthony challenged. Altruism was hard for him to understand. Instinct suggested deception. A part of him suspected that Raven meant every word she said. Any crisis could be profitable, if he could just see the angle.

"Heat of the moment," Ness said admiringly in an effort to break the tension. "Anger. Misunderstanding. The new boss pleads lack of knowledge. Our unofficial arrangement becomes null and void because she made a mistake that gets swept under the rug."

Frost leaned toward Siggs conspiratorially. "Naturally, you'd be replaced by a new generation of...whatever you guys like to call yourselves. My security forces can't be everywhere, so we'd make a new deal. Not as good as the old arrangement you're so familiar with, but still...beneficial to whoever might be in this room at the time."

Anthony looked to Wanda, who signaled her consent. Nobody else at the table made a sound. "We seem to have a majority," he conceded, "Well, then...Deputy. I agree to your terms. With one condition of my own."

Raven moved back in her seat. "I can be reasonable."

Siggs licked his drying lips. “We’ve never taken sides quite like this,” he fidgeted. “It may take ‘em a few days to figure it out, but they will. When they do, certain parties will have it in for us. Probably means no foreign travel and, quite possibly, a few unexplained accidents here at the starport.”

“Hazards of the life you chose.”

Anthony raised his voice when his underlings began to protest. “Civilian travel documents and resident permits for the families of everyone in this room, so they can live here or relocate!” he demanded.

“You’re not bringing trouble to my starport!” Raven dissented. “We’ll turn a blind eye to anyone who wants to leave. If you and all of your relations go somewhere else, I will personally wipe the slate clean so you can try living an honest life. That’s the best you get.”

“None of us can do that!”

Raven pointed at the door she’d come through by jerking a thumb over her shoulder. “There’s a hundred people out there swilling lousy beer, trying to get by on less than you have,” she replied forcefully. “I’ve got more than a thousand people on white collar payroll that came from places like this. Don’t tell me it can’t be done until you’ve tried.”

“We don’t have to take this!” somebody whispered.

“Hush!” Wanda commanded.

Siggs scanned the faces of everyone present, as if reading their minds. “Nobody likes your terms,” he concluded, “but we have no real alternatives. Okay *Deputy*, we’ll play it your way this time. How long is your safe passage good for?”

“Thirty days,” Raven promised, pushing her chair back. “Any of you and your relations who fly or float your way out of here do so with my blessing—as long as you do it through official channels. Don’t vanish. Disappear, and I’ll send what we have on you to every law enforcement agency on this planet, regardless of jurisdiction."

"You're difficult to work with," Siggs grinned.

"No, I'm not," Frost replied tartly while getting to her feet. She walked out without saying another word.

Arguments began among faction leaders before the door was fully closed. "I like her," Wanda said to Siggs with a mixture of respect and loathing when the future starport boss was gone, "She might end up like her predecessor, but I *do* like her."

* * *

Raven made her way out of the busy bar, taking a different route back to the monorail station. She fell in with a group of fast-walking workers who talked among themselves about rushing to catch the next train.

"I can't be late again," she pretended to gripe in an effort to fit in.

"They're using anything as an excuse to let us go," a blustering woman dressed for office work complained.

Frost took note of their complaints as each person sounded off.

"I know times are tough," she followed along. "This is getting a little ridiculous."

"Pressure comes off when we can fly again," a large man wearing a scarred parka guessed while they jogged down an empty escalator staircase. "Wouldn't surprise me if they're bleeding cash to keep jobs."

Raven waited for the man to walk by so she could read the name sewn on his coat when they reached the ground floor lobby. "What makes you think they're smart enough to do that?"

"We're still going to work!" another woman in food service garb laughed while searching her purse for a prepaid boarding pass.

Frost waited her turn in line as everyone went through a turnstile on the electronic gate, which deducted the fare from each passenger's media or electronic device. She was pleased to hear what amounted to a vote of confidence, in spite of what she'd already seen in other parts of Boom Town. She found a seat in an unoccupied section of one car and rode through a dozen stops before arriving at a pre-arranged commercial terminal where she hoped to meet Billy.

Raven strolled slowly out of the foul-smelling monorail with some relief. She was flagged down by a beaming Richter, who sat behind the steering wheel of a low-slung bright yellow electric cart. "I told you it would be a quick meeting," he smirked while zipping a light jacket that hid his rank and other insignias.

CHAPTER EIGHT

The launch coordinator stood under the bright lights at the foot of the administrator's dais, waving a remote control in each hand. Local television stations continued broadcasting reaction to Billy Richter's comments about the recent demise of Administrator Cook and his entourage.

"Motorists are advised to avoid this part of town so that ambulances can get through."

"Firefighters have cleared lanes for pumper trucks to reach water mains."

Beatrice Brown remained calm as a commercial segment ended. She smiled into the nearest camera as her next segment began. "Welcome back to Starport News. We're continuing our live coverage of this evening's tragedy that's unfolding in downtown Anchorage."

Radio chatter in the coordinator's headset told him that the facility was nearing full readiness. "Air defense reports Gatekeeper approaching altitude," a voice told him as Raven entered the high ceilinged chamber, dressed as she had been before, with Billy Richter and two specialists close behind.

"Deputy on deck!" Andre shouted.

"All departments report," Frost commanded.

Allison handed her a tablet computer as she approached. "Combat air patrol is on station in four minutes. Nanook finishes fueling in six minutes."

Raven took the device she was offered and turned to Billy. "Send one of your people to my office. Have them look for a package of some kind on my desk. Might be an envelope. Bring it to me."

"Do it," Richter said to the man behind him.

Andre pointed at the pad in Frost's hand. "Disciplinary matter. The senior aviation ordnance handler has logged a notation you should be aware of. Lieutenant Connor Beck somehow appropriated four restricted weapons."

"That would be Norman's doing," Billy whispered as his subordinate rushed out of sight. "He broke protocol because you wouldn't let him have those items."

Frost looked at the computer in her hand, then at Billy. "I've heard stories about his father. Insubordination runs in the family."

"What are you going to do about it?"

Raven entered her executive authority code to erase the disciplinary report. "Mr. Beck won't pay for the sins of his squadron commander…this time. I gave the order for terrestrial aviation to fly when there was a high probability of aerospace threat. Anyone with a tap on our official communications will have every reason to believe those pilots are up there with nothing more than conventional weapons. Why spoil a perfectly good surprise?"

"Yes, ma'am," Andre agreed before going quickly to another workstation where a group of men and women appeared to be waiting for him.

"Slick," Billy said admiringly.

"You guys break enough rules to get yourselves fired at least once a month."

"Don't be so quick to judge," he cautioned while tugging at his uniform to smooth out a few obvious wrinkles. "Difficult jobs require difficult solutions."

Raven turned her attention to the computer in her hands, flicking through pages of data. "I should remember that when I have to break a few rules? Is that what you're telling me?"

"Of course."

"Excuse me," a female voice interrupted politely.

Frost looked up to see a well-dressed woman in a burgundy pantsuit with a matching briefcase. "Deputy," the formal emissary began, "My name is Jane Martell. I've brought some things that need your attention."

"Can this wait?" Frost wanted to know while raising her tablet. "We're in the middle of something rather complicated and I just don't have time for bureaucracy."

"I've come from Human Resources with your promotion," the attorney explained.

"This isn't what I was told to expect."

Martell clasped both hands over the handle of her expensive satchel. "Official channels have been somewhat disrupted. I'm what you might call a backup plan. Only to be called in extreme situations. May we proceed? This will only take a moment."

Raven gave her tablet to Billy. "Remember what we talked about? Please have this taken care of." Richter read the small display before turning to his aide. "Frank, she wants us to have deep data storage inspected one more time," he whispered as Frost conferred with the lawyer on the dais. "Double the guard on those levels and deny access to the interior compartments for the next 24 hours."

"I'll handle this in person," the subordinate suggested after reading from the tablet in Billy's hand. "No radios. No logs. Nothing that telegraphs our vigilance to eavesdroppers."

Billy watched his trusted lieutenant leave. He was about to find his own way out when the night shift coordinator caught his attention with a wave. The security chief chuckled. "You're going to do that now?"

"Would you?" the supervisor snickered while smoothing out his necktie.

Richter looked at the raised platform and folded his arms. "Yes, I would."

* * *

"Sign here, here, and initial here," Jane pointed over Raven's shoulder.

The executive scanned each printed page with practiced ease before writing her name with a ballpoint pen imprinted with the starport logo. "Says here I have ten days to name my replacement as deputy," she paraphrased. "I thought the board made those decisions?"

"Emergency provision," Martell clarified. "Been on the books for a long time. I've never seen this option used before, so I guess they're going to see just how good your judgment really is."

"My choice?" Raven repeated.

"Yours."

Frost filled in her initials with a flourish and sat back. The lawyer sent a short text message using her wireless phone and collected the signed documents with a genuine smile. "Congratulations, you're the first female starport boss on Planet Earth!"

Loud applause caused Raven and her counsel to look in Billy's direction. Launch coordinator Andre Allison bounded up the steps of the dais as a crowd gathered. "It's time for you to have this," he announced momentously, handing over a black jewelry box.

"Every senior gets one," the lawyer prompted.

"I know that," Frost remarked with growing embarrassment. She opened the box to reveal an obsolete stainless steel timepiece with hour, minute, and second hands on a silver chain link wristband. "I just didn't expect to be doing this right now," Raven fussed.

"You have no sense of history!" Billy jeered.

The newly promoted executive got to her feet, showing off the ceremonial totem by sweeping it around in a wide arc so that most of the spectators could see the open box. "Thanks very much for this," she bowed with a flushed face. "We've still got a problem in motion, so let's get back to work!"

* * *

High above the Bering Sea, a modified 747 studded with antenna blisters and sensor domes banked into a shallow turn to avoid an approaching storm front that obscured some of the constellations that would have otherwise been visible in the night sky. Exterior midsection lighting on either side of the long fuselage illuminated a Kodiak starport logo, causing the ascending surveillance platform to be easily locatable as it climbed through 60,000 feet.

Twenty-four modified F-15s in mottled blue camouflage with starport insignias on their twin tail fins easily escorted the slower-moving civilian airliner in a split-level formation that enveloped it at a distance of five miles. Directional transmitters inside the wide hull turned east, toward Kodiak Island, as onboard computers sought and found a coded navigation signal sent from the busy starport that was used throughout the region by aircraft and vessels at sea. Cockpit radios squawked with chatter as the flight crew attended to their duties.

"Gatekeeper is on station," the pilot announced.

Digital camera systems scanned the sky and peered down at the ocean. Software sifted real-time images to search for anything that wasn't authorized to be there as the jumbo jet reached 100,000 feet.

"Assume high guard and contact sentry flight on prearranged frequency," the night shift coordinator cut in to order. "Start your sweep soonest. Office pool says company's coming."

"Position verified," an air defense specialist acknowledged from the comfort of the underground mission control complex. "LOS established. Lidar can see you. Data feeds are active, to and from. Show us what you see."

Optical and thermal filters zeroed in on the nighttime glow from a dozen facilities in and around the starport as lights that shone through the darkness and scattered cloud cover. Images were sent back to the starport with a two-second delay for encryption. They were decoded and analyzed by a newly created information analysis unit that worked deep underground.

Technicians onboard the repurposed cargo plane began conversing with their ground-based counterparts while sensors in the airplanes and on Kodiak Island began to probe the heavens for the presence of moving manmade objects.

"Compensate for atmospheric refraction."

"Wreckage. Particulates. Debris tracks."

"All the usual trash," somebody clowned.

"Maybe they're not coming?" another voice doubted.

* * *

"We've been on full alert for a while now," Andre advised Raven from where he stood. Aviation data filled a dozen small screens on her workstation. "It's just on 3 a.m. I'd like to begin rest rotations."

The newly appointed senior administrator adjusted the fit of her gleaming wristwatch without looking up. "Relieve air defense first," she said, thinking out loud. "Gatekeeper is starting the outbound portion of its patrol now. Where's Billy?"

"Still here!" Richter piped up from a nearby chair with a telephone in his hand.

"Have you done what I asked?" she prompted.

"All underground sites are accounted for," he affirmed while continuing to listen to a voice on the phone. "Deep data storage is being inspected now, extra guards will be in place within five minutes."

"Reduce area lighting," she told Allison. "By the way, who is your Number Two? I'd like to have a few words with them, just to be sure we're all on the same page, pages, or library."

"He's where I'd like to be," Andre replied with a thin smirk while using an interface on his tablet computer to dim the overhead lights. "Sorry. Out of line. Most of the department seniors are out of town or in other parts of the state right now, having their Christmas vacation."

"It's okay," Raven decided, knowing that every word she said would be overheard. "This will give the juniors a chance to see what it's like to run the show. A lot of what happens next is out of our hands. All we can do is wait for it."

"Suppose the analysts are wrong and the event we're defending against isn't an aerospace attack?" he asked.

Frost looked at the nearest ceiling-mounted television screen and the silent image of Beatrice Brown, who was recapping the official version of events that were still playing out in the streets of Anchorage. "They won't send bombers, drones, or warships into our conventional air defense radius because of our past bad behavior," she reasoned sarcastically. "Submarines are too busy hunting each other, so that leaves just two choices—long-range missiles or a kinetic strike of some kind from low orbit. A small nudge from us is all it takes to skew the odds, so they'll prefer the aerospace option."

Andre refrained from voicing further doubts while a team of engineers moved around him with bulky equipment.

Raven pointed at the ceiling with one hand while continuing to watch three different computer screens on her desk. "What do you see?" she asked without looking up.

"Brown," he shrugged, "She's yakking about missile defense again."

"Every chance she gets for the last two years," Raven mumbled as if that bit of trivia didn't matter.

Andre made room for another pair of technicians who hurried by with a monitor mount trailing a tangled mess of cables. "Repeat something until it sounds like the truth," the supervisor said thoughtfully, smiling mischievously. "How can you be sure this is going to work?"

Frost briefly glanced at her gleaming watch before spearing the coordinator with her full attention. "We'll know soon enough."

Nearby movement caught her eye. The arrival of Richter's courier caused Raven's enthusiasm to rise. "What have you got for me?"

"There was no secretary so I just went in," he explained while approaching the dais to hand the administrator a sealed white envelope with something in it. "This was in your chair."

Frost took the envelope and ripped it open as the man stepped back to confer with Billy. A small, black, plastic rectangle with a silver metal connector fell into her outstretched hand. She looked over shoulders to be sure that she was alone on the platform before plugging the memory stick into a data port. Several screens on her workstation lit up with charts, diagrams, and text.

"Billy! Come up here and have a look."

The security chief told his aide to have a seat and bounded up the steps of the dais to stand beside the administrator. "So." He squinted while bending over to survey the screens she pointed at. "Are you buying this?"

Raven tapped one of the facility maps on display, "Of course not. The important thing is what they're not showing us. Here, here, and here," she emphasized with an index finger. "It's what any criminal would do under these conditions."

"You can hardly blame them."

Frost looked up at him disparagingly. "That's a conversation for some other time," she commented acerbically. "*If* we correctly guessed their method of attack, and *if* they fall for our deception, we'll have that chance to stop this crazy thing."

Billy stood up straight. "There has been so much negative reaction to the Tokyo incident," he speculated with one hand over his mouth to stifle a yawn, "temping them with a spur-of-the-moment chance to hit us in a way that isn't absolutely end-of-the-world lethal might be hard for any politician to resist."

"That's what I'm counting on," Raven replied. "If it sounds too good to be true, they'll just go on ahead with whatever they were going to do. All of our defenses are up and running, so—"

"Yeah," Richter interjected, "I should go. They'll be up to no good by now, if they're going to sell us out. Just remember what I told you earlier."

"Which was?"

Billy walked quickly down the steps of the dais. "Difficult jobs require difficult solutions. That's why we break the rules."

CHAPTER NINE

The Chinese aerospace strike force reached the highest point of its trajectory. An absence of sophisticated detection systems in low orbit allowed all three space planes to fly unnoticed through airspace claimed by the Russian and American governments as they raced over the North Pole. Fewer pieces of debris struck the space planes at this latitude. All of the experienced pilots were moved by the panorama they saw while changing course.

* * *

Raven's encounter at The Bloody Bucket resulted in a series of not-so-subtle inquiries made by Siggs and his associates that were easily detected by Chinese security and intelligence agencies. The general physical location of most major industrial assets within the boundaries of any starport was never in doubt, though accurate dispositions were always hard to come by.

Frost's interest in the specific location of Jiuquan's deep data storage sparked a debate in the Central Committee. This led to a sudden interest in the location of Kodiak Starport's underground computer depot, which could render that launch complex just as temporarily inactive as Jiuquan could be, if it was significantly damaged or destroyed by aerospace attack. Analysts had very little time to consider the pros and cons of what appeared to be an opening move on the part of Kodiak's new administrator. A.I. simulation and human guesswork led politicians and planners alike to believe that her response to the devastation of Tokyo's starport was incrementally defensive.

"There's no fear in this," a respected observer told his audience behind closed doors, "We've done a lot to earn a very massive response from the Kodiak Starport, if they are attacked by us. They are sending a signal that means just one thing. No escalation, if we make certain choices."

* * *

The phrase "deep data storage" was more than shorthand for subterranean electronics. These carefully guarded underground bunkers contained expensive computers and hard-to-come-by spare parts that would be used to rebuild shattered networks. Centralization was a blend of technology, philosophy, and politics that depended on the nature of the government or corporation that built and maintained them.

Central Committee leaders in Beijing were provided with reaction assessments based on the professional profiles of known Kodiak Starport personnel. They skimmed printed pages and social media profiles while being updated on the progress of their aerospace strike force. Worldwide reaction to events in Japan weighed more heavily on some than others. A "soft kill" seemed preferable to complete ruin as they conferred with each other through secured phone and video.

"Administrator Frost is calling for restraint," an outspoken member from the North concluded. "We must assume she has an option to back up her position."

Military advisors representing every branch of service dissented, making the case for total ruin of the Kodiak complex, even if that meant loss of invaluable facilities. "This has become more than a question of terrestrial force dominance. Control of space determines more than victory on the ground. The nation that maintains that supremacy will choose who among their neighbors does, or doesn't, share that prosperity."

The decision to acquire strategic details from Kodiak Starport's criminal element was made with approval from skeptical intelligence experts, who had every intention of reciprocating with disinformation in the hopes of receiving something useful from an unscrupulous source. Leadership at all levels agreed that this spur-of-the-moment risk was worth taking. Verbal and physical transactions were completed in a matter of seconds as criminal cartels in the Jiuquan and Kodiak Starports exchanged money and materials with each other through a time-honored network of intermediaries.

* * *

According to the questionable specs Raven got from Anthony Siggs, Jiuquan appeared to have three widely separated computer vaults, located under civilian structures, in soft sedimentary rock surrounded by steel-reinforced concrete. Aerospace planners in Beijing were told about Kodiak's single massive storage site, located beneath a layer of dense sedimentary bedrock.

"Difficult," an ordnance expert determined when informed of the target, "Two penetrators, one after the other—at speed from high altitude—will go subterranean like a hot knife through butter."

* * *

The inbound Chinese pilots were not surprised when their list of approved targets changed. Each space plane received encrypted data, sent from an airplane similar to Kodiak's "Gatekeeper," through a receiver in its tail. That command-and-control platform cruised at a very high altitude in Chinese airspace so that it could send burst transmissions to the aerospace fighters before they disappeared over the horizon.

Revisions included orders to attack Kodiak Starport's underground data storage site. The trio of jets assumed a single file formation as new attack procedures were discussed through heavily encrypted radio frequencies.

Automated navigation systems performed flawlessly, each vehicle completing its assigned turn and burn after a few simple inputs from its human pilot. All three aviators worked through checklists that changed their direction of attack without adversely affecting fuel consumption. They avoided any casual speculation, knowing that every word they said would be recorded and reviewed by somebody in a position of authority at a later date.

* * *

Surveillance satellites still active in high orbit observed their passing and reported portions of their sensor data to ground stations through interference from orbiting debris that blocked their transmissions. Fragmentary information reaching earthbound receivers was routed through bureaucratic channels for evaluation. Human analysts who viewed it in real time had mixed opinions. Most determined what they saw to be "a supersonic aircraft transit, destination unknown," while a few warned that these fast moving contacts might be an aerospace attack bound for Kodiak Island.

* * *

Norman Ahgupuk looked down through his digital helmet display at the illuminated fuselage of the 747 that his squadron was escorting. The view from his chilly cockpit was majestic as he watched the distant jet begin its southbound turn high above a sparkling moonlit sea. Warmth flowed to his arms and legs through electrically heated boots, gloves, and flight suit.

"Gatekeeper reports horizon contact!" the defense manager aboard the big jet called out through a priority scrambled frequency, "Sentry flight to high guard. Starport, assume readiness condition Red-One and standby for threat identification!"

Ahgupuk read his instruments while changing radio frequencies. "Elements One and Two, climb to first position. Element Three, mind the store. Wide perimeter. Section leaders, form up on me."

Voices acknowledged orders as F-15s moved. Two groups of seven airplanes roared higher into the night, while a third seven-ship formation spread out ahead of the lumbering 747 in a crescent-shaped arc. Norman and his three section leaders adopted a wedge formation as their supercharged aircraft climbed even higher in to the thin atmosphere, to the limit of their operational ceiling.

"Sentry Leader, what are you doing?" the air defense manager asked.

Norman cleared his throat. "Call my element Special Delivery," he suggested cheerfully. "We are loaded for orbital intercept. Ready to receive your telemetry."

"I have no clearance for this," the defense manager objected.

"Better get some."

"Seriously?" a technician aboard Gatekeeper whispered incredulously.

Ahgupuk responded glibly, "If I'm right, your sensors are looking at an inbound aerospace threat. Tell your gadgets to shake hands with our gizmos, so we can do something about it!"

Raven Frost interrupted through a burst of static as her signal was beamed from the starport to the distant 747 through a developing rainstorm. "This is Administrator One-One," she announced forcefully. "Establish remote links and prosecute those targets!"

"We'll have to verify—"

"Stop talking to me and do it!" she commanded.

* * *

Computers onboard "Gatekeeper" operated software that interpreted information as it was gathered by sensors on the skin of the aircraft. All three partial radar contacts were tracked by radar and lidar. They were also scrutinized by digital optics as they sped over the horizon into full view of the 747's detection equipment.

Human specialists made split-second decisions based on what they read from their workstation displays. Target classification took no more than two seconds as the well-trained crew worked through flexible procedures that left very little room for doubt.

"Classified. Inbound is low-visibility military aerospace," the defense manager told his terrestrial colleagues. "Minimal radar returns and infrared signatures indicate stealth, or what's left of it. Note the scatter from what appears to be the central fuselage? Looks like they've been eating some wreckage on their way over the pole. I'm designating them as Aggressor-One, Two, and Three."

Raven listened from her dais as range and location information about the incoming aerospace vehicles was fed to Norman's climbing F-15s. She turned to deal with more complex tasks while the anti-satellite missiles tucked under the wings of each old jet woke up.

* * *

"Air defense warning!" an automated voice announced through loudspeakers above and below ground. "This is not a training exercise or a drill. All employees, report to your duty stations. Civilians, please go to the nearest emergency accommodation."

* * *

Administrator Frost watched department reports flow onto her workstation displays with some satisfaction. "Good reaction times," she complimented.

"Nothing like on the job experience," the night shift coordinator joked from his position ten feet away.

The apprehensive woman appraised what she could see from her elevation position. "How much of this do we have plugged in?" she wondered.

"Eighty percent," he quoted from memory.

"Very good," she replied approvingly, brushing dark hair out of her eyes. Radio chatter filled Raven's ear as she used a touch screen to manually select a secure communications channel to the starport's news division.

"Control room," Kyle Foss answered. "What can I do for you Mrs. Frost?"

"We're about to be attacked by Chinese aerospace fighters," she told him quietly.

"Really?"

"Wouldn't kid about a thing like that," she scolded.

"How soon?" he wondered.

"Any time now," she hinted.

"Are you sure?" Foss quizzed while alerting his producers. "Did anyone know this could happen?"

"Can you hear the sirens?" Raven hassled just to keep him on topic.

"Yeah, but when did—"

"Don't hype," Frost raised her voice. "Work from the surface-level camera feeds and use what you get from other networks. Some really good freelancers are flying drones in our area. Brown has an eye for that sort of thing. Let her buy some of their video when it comes up for sale; I'll back any purchase within reason. Blood and gore gets ratings, but I have a memo from legal asking us to avoid anything that shows off mass casualties!"

"Can we have cockpit video?" he asked eagerly.

Uncensored air combat could be a tremendously valuable source of public relations imagery.

Subscription charges and advertising fees generated from such pay-per-view events could be worth hundreds of millions of dollars. Audiences watching such spectacles live, without very many commercial interruptions, could be persuaded to think more positively of the government or company that sponsored the feed.

"Not this time," Raven disallowed.

"We'll be missing—"

She made an authoritative noise. "You've got a ringside seat for the world's first bombing from space!" she barked. "You can't be any closer to the action *because we are the target.* Make the most of every ground-level camera angle you've got and hope they spell your name right in the history books."

The senior administrator hung up with a swipe of her finger over a touch screen. Verbalizing new commands, she called the starport's aerospace controller.

"Mission ready," he told her after she completed a complex authentication procedure. "All four ships are fueled and loaded with strike packages."

"Saddle up," Frost ordered with more confidence than she felt.

"Location is Jiuquan," the officer affirmed while reading mission details from a nearby display. "What are the specific targets?"

"I'll give them to you when it's time to go," she asserted before ending the conversation.

* * *

G-forces pushed Norman Ahgupuk deep into his ejection seat as his F-15 strained to reach its maximum altitude. Conventional jet engines in the rear of each fighter were powered down and shut off by the skilled pilots as they "choked out."

Rocket pods attached to underwing pylons on each aircraft were then ignited to further propel them through a shallow arc that would briefly grant them more altitude. As practiced, Norman and the officers who followed him would attack the oncoming formation of aerospace vehicles with their anti-satellite missiles when they momentarily slowed down at the top of their arching climb, before beginning a hazardous descent to Earth. That brief interval of "hang time" would last less than a tenth of a second, during which many computers would make decisions that no human could. The result would mean life or death as the fast moving formations passed each other on the edge of space.

* * *

Mechanics, assisted by robots, worked through final engine checks under bright lights inside Kodiak Starport's underground aerospace hangar. Ordnance loading was completed while computer-toting technicians argued about last minute instrument settings.

Pilots with recent combat experience in modern jet fighters walked to their planes in brightly colored vacuum suits similar to those worn by American astronauts. Dark sun visors were pulled down on wide-rimmed helmets to hide faces from a dozen circling male and female camera operators who worked in the bitter cold to capture history in high definition video.

"Over here," one of the shivering videographers shouted. "Look this way, please!"

Squadron patches, military emblems, state flags, and national insignia that adorned the outer shells of their repurposed flight suits were hard to see in the shifting spotlights. No name tags were worn by any of the aviators who climbed into the middle of the wide, teardrop-shaped hulls. If they lived, they'd be famous—assuming anyone ever found out who they were.

"Thirty second warning!" a synthetic voice announced through overhead speakers. "Discontinue fueling. Engine start in 30 seconds. Technicians, leave the apron."

* * *

"Approaching apogee," Norman announced as wing-mounted booster rockets on all four aircraft shut off. "Top of the arch in five seconds. Changing call sign. Designate Sentry Leader as Intercept-A. Designate the rest of my formation accordingly."

Voices aboard Gatekeeper called out course corrections. The rapidly realigning group of warplanes spread out in a staggered cell to improve their chances of engaging the inbound force. The action would later be analyzed as a single pass, merge-and-shoot encounter. In spite of past preparation, none of the fighter pilots had any illusions about their chances for success. Extreme speed and the fact that their higher and faster opponent still had the advantage of partial stealth meant they were literally shooting in the dark.

"Readiness check," Norman requested as his formation reached the top of its powerless trajectory.

All four aviators in Ahgupuk's hastily organized combat group reported positively on their preparations as remotely controlled ordnance management systems, operated by technicians aboard Gatekeeper, were tied in to the anti-satellite missiles. They reflexively scanned the darkness around them for threats none of them would've been able to do anything about, even if they had been able to see them. Penetrating cold combined with an unfamiliar feeling brought on by prolonged weightlessness to make all of them feel uneasy as the pull of gravity forced them to slow down.

"Firing point!" an unseen technician announced as the formation's forward momentum peaked.

"Release!" the defense manager broadcast as each remotely controlled missile roared to life. Rocket motors flared as all four weapons raced away from the descending jets.

"Tally ho!" Norman joked as the glare of each rocket's exhaust faded from view.

CHAPTER TEN

Sensors in the nose and fuselage of each inbound aerospace fighter registered radar and laser emissions being sent out from the starport's command and control aircraft as they raced over the horizon and into full view of the 747 and its escorts. All three pilots had something humorous to say as threat warnings flickered on and off inside their helmet displays. Despite what was clearly its best effort, the entire American formation of fighters—and its high guard element—was still too low in the atmosphere to engage them with any degree of accuracy.

Years of simulated engagements and real-world training had convinced the pilots and tacticians of many nations that space planes would outperform their terrestrial counterparts by such a wide margin that they'd be invincible in any future conflict. Designers determined that speed and stealth would negate the tactical requirement for defensive air-to-air weapons.

* * *

Kyle Foss watched three different clocks and a dozen monitors while bellowing at producers and assistants in the television studio when they were close enough to be seen. He shouted through his multichannel headset as they sorted through long-range images of Gatekeeper and the F-15s that swarmed around the zigzagging 747. Intermittent cloud cover obscured all of the aircraft, making it hard for the digital cameras around the starport to view them clearly. "Let me know when we have ten seconds for a clean loop," he demande

Beatrice Brown settled into her seat. Bright overhead lighting softened as logos faded on every display to signal an end to the commercial break. "Welcome back," she began professionally. "Hostile forces are approaching our location at extremely high altitude. Video feed is on delay from ground-based camera stations here at the Kodiak Starport to avoid showing you anything that might compromise area defenses."

Still photos showcasing people, places, and equipment appeared in the background above the anchorwoman as she continued to describe what was being streamed onto the internet for public viewing. "Cloud cover and darkness make it hard for our cameras to see the jet fighters that are protecting this facility," she lied. "Even so, we're going to show you what we can. Please bear in mind that thousands of lives are at risk. What you're about see may not be suitable for younger viewers."

* * *

Strident warnings rang out when missile launches were observed. Onboard computers determined that the 747 had remotely programmed the ASMs with a firing solution that had a low kill probability. Colonel Liu Tao refrained from ordering an increase in speed or a change in course because none of the rapidly approaching weapons were likely to hit any of his planes.

"Going to be close," Major Deng Bao observed from the middle of the formation.

Captain Yin Zhuo swore when it seemed he might be unlucky.

* * *

Each of the accelerating anti-satellite missiles turned on its own nose-mounted sensors when it lost contact with Gatekeeper's long distance data stream. Though smaller and less capable than the versions carried by the starport's upgraded 747, they required less than a second after launch to find what they were looking for as the F-15s began their descent.

Miniaturized radars, lidars and digital optics in each missile located some trace of the aerospace fighters in front of them. Thrusters in the tail and sides of each missile twisted or turned to change the ASM's angle of approach as its internal computer revised its navigation calculations. Identification programs checked and rechecked optical images to be sure the Chinese craft were "real." Although they operated independently, each preprogrammed platform made such similar decisions that they appeared to act in unison.

Veering sharply upward in a sudden rush, all four missiles flew into the path of the trailing aerospace fighter before exploding in a hailstorm of steel buckshot that spread out in an expanding cloud of tiny metal spheres.

One of those shrapnel patterns blossomed in front of Captain Zhuo's fighter. Thousands of ball bearings tore through the nose, fuselage, and wings of the hypersonic craft as it slammed into the comparatively slow torrent of metal. Sudden loss of aerodynamic integrity threw the space plane in to a high-g spin.

Yin passed out as his cockpit was perforated by ball bearings and small, sharp pieces of the ship's outer hull. He was crushed inside his rapidly shredding vacuum suit before his vehicle disintegrated in a fiery blaze of spiraling wreckage.

* * *

Dozens of cameras on pylons and turrets throughout the starport observed a high altitude explosion on the western horizon. The imagery was presented to increasing audiences as a brief smear of bright light in the night sky that was momentarily visible through cloud cover. Thermal imaging capability allowed some digital systems to see larger pieces of sparkling wreckage as they plunged toward the Bering Sea. Low resolution variants of each approved feed were prepared by technicians before being introduced by Beatrice Brown.

"That bright flash of light you're seeing in the center of our skycam display is an indication of high altitude air combat," she explained. The stress in her voice grew as graphics featuring stock footage of starport F-15s danced in the background. "It's all moving very fast. Employees here at the starport have been ordered to their worksites. Civilians have been asked to find the nearest emergency shelter and stay there. Security forces are on full alert. No matter what happens next, I'm going to stay on the air."

* * *

Both of the remaining Chinese aerospace fighters broke formation to evade approaching debris from their trailing craft. Accelerating on plumes of blue flame that were barely visible to the naked eye, the experienced pilots manually programmed new attack patterns into their navigation computers. The adaptive software responded quickly.

The senior officer remained focused on the task at hand. "Four seconds to drop point," he warned. "Switch to secondary target set. We can still get the job done."

"Weapon priorities reassigned," his subordinate acknowledged with cold brevity as the distance between them increased. "Good luck to you, sir!"

The attackers changed course once more to approach the Kodiak Starport from slightly different directions. Computers opened internal storage bays, dropping a pair of 6,000-pound rods from each ship as they passed over their release points. All six self-guiding packages began to seek their destinations while the aerospace fighters departed. Each of the kinetic strike weapons used multi-spectrum digital optics and object recognition systems to find landmarks on the ground. These aim points were used to zero in on vital starport infrastructure hidden underground. Falling from extremely high altitude encouraged gravity to propel each rod of dense metal through rock and dirt at supersonic speeds. The resulting impacts damaged or destroyed whatever the rods burrowed through, to a depth of several hundred yards.

* * *

Emergency lighting flashed or glowed as sirens wailed throughout the battle-ready complex. Manmade thunderclaps announced the staggered activation of ground-based air defenses, filling the night with a mixture of ballistic and missile-delivered shrapnel.

Control surfaces on the descending projectiles changed shape as needed to alter their aerodynamics, causing them to change their angle of approach. They plunged through miles of atmosphere, passing unharmed through layers of flak designed to confuse or destroy conventional heat-seeking missiles.

"Kinetic strike inbound!" Gatekeeper's air defense manager warned.

"Shut down all nonessential electronic networks!" Raven Frost ordered from her dais. She activated emergency lighting in the operations center that changed overhead illumination from an industrial white to a soft red, quietly saying a prayer for anyone still in harm's way.

Monitors on her desk showed live color images of the starport's aerospace fighters taxiing down long, dimly lit passages. Each plane was being escorted by a large six-wheeled flatbed crane with flashing red and blue lights that would be used to load it onto an underground catapult. That launch mechanism would propel each ship along a protected runway on a rocket sled that would fling it into the air at sea level, allowing each to zoom skyward through a tunnel exit at supersonic speed.

* * *

Audiences around the world watched the ground shake as Kodiak Starport facilities rocked on their earthquake-resistant foundations. All four Chinese weapons slammed into their assigned locations with enough brute force to trigger seismic warnings at monitoring stations across the Asia-Pacific Rim. Dust and debris filled the air, blotting out the night vision capability of most of the cameras that were being used to support the real-time appearance of Brown's commentary.

"We've been attacked!" she observed nervously as fixtures around her jumped and rattled. "I'm not sure what just happened, but you saw it. Can we go to commercial? I need a minute to find somebody who can tell us more. Yes? Okay, then. We'll be right back with more live coverage of this showdown at the Kodiak Starport."

* * *

"How bad?" Frost asked worriedly as workstations around her went dark.

Voices chimed in from all directions as reports began to appear on her monitors.

"Deep data storage, as expected."

"Electrical generation. Multiple turbines hit."

"Rocket fuel plant. Explosions. Fire. Emergency services responding."

Raven surveyed the incoming information at a glance, while turning to take in the mood of the people around her. “Aerospace readiness?” she demanded of anyone who would answer. “What about the catapults and runways?”

“No hits!” Andre shouted through a rising tide of voices and active telephones.

Frost was pleased to see very few faces looking in her direction. Most of the men and women were focused on their own jobs or helping each other deal with something as the ground under their feet continued to shake.

Conscious of her own anger and the fearful onlookers who did need direction, the senior administrator stood up to her full height, knowing that the dais would add to her stature. “It’s been a long night and I’ve had enough,” she asserted through the area intercom. “Nobody bombs my starport and gets away with it! Everybody—all of you—reset the boards and let’s fight back!”

CHAPTER ELEVEN

Outrage over the nuclear devastation of Japan and the loss of Tokyo's urban launch facility was still dominating mainstream infotainment air time when commentators got word of the attack on Alaska's Kodiak Starport. Ongoing coverage of the fires raging in downtown Anchorage became part of the increasingly complicated backstory as multinational franchises brought their audiences more of Beatrice Brown's post-combat narration.

* * *

A series of explosions at the rocket fuel refinery shook Kodiak Island for miles in all directions, causing dust to fall from the ceiling of the underground operations center. Emergency lighting bathed the area in soft red as men and women went about the assigned duties.

"Casualties?" Raven asked worriedly from her dais.

"Plant supervisor reports two," Andre responded, reading from a handheld device. "Half the complex is now on battery backup. Whatever you're going to do, you've got about 12 hours to make it happen. After that, all major systems are—"

"I know," she replied, cutting him off. Through the color monitors on her desk, she saw the last of four multirole aerospace fighters loaded onto a rocket-assisted catapult by workers wearing insulated suits and boots with heavy gloves and long hoods.

A chime sounded. "Aerospace control," Raphe Chandler announced in her ear, "Showtime in 30 minutes. We're just checking. Do you want to revise any of those target specs?"

Raven thought about the information she'd leveraged from Siggs. There was no reason to assume he or any member of his cartel would be truthful, even if it meant ensuring their own safety. Anything they passed on to her about locations inside Jiuquan Starport would be false or intended to mislead. Knowing that, she could still make an educated guess about where some vital structures were likely to be, based on what the allegedly "real" specifications claimed.

"Sending revised Jiuquan targets now," she told him, working through a series of menus on different screens. "You should be seeing them now."

"That's a very long flight. Are you sure about this?"

"I want them to see us coming," she chuckled.

He cringed when more coordinates appeared. "Over the North Pole, down to the South Pole—just to be flashy? Even with extra fuel, that's askin' for trouble. Would you like to come down here and sign one of the rods?"

"Too busy," Raven replied tersely.

"A more direct route through Japanese airspace would be safe!" he objected.

"Tell Mr. Allison when final checks are complete and wait for my order."

* * *

Ambulances rushed through the early morning darkness to every corner of the starport, escorted by armed security units. Lights and sirens announced their arrival at scenes of carnage and chaos, where impact craters had been gouged deep into the frozen earth. Some holes were more like trenches, swallowing whole buildings or complexes.

Light snow fell as paramedics and volunteers searched for the injured. Security specialists swept the surrounding areas for suspicious persons and unattended packages that might contain booby traps or spy gear. Firefighters were sent to battle the most aggressive blazes that threatened irreplaceable or highly combustible structures. Everything else was allowed to burn.

Low light cameras in and around the affected areas provided starport security and media reps with objective views of the unfolding situation. Some feeds were used to look for people who were up to no good, like known criminals who might be trying to take advantage of the situation. Others were chosen to provide news organizations around the world with live images that would be later be closely examined by conspiracy theorists.

* * *

Raven walked into the busy broadcast studio ten minutes later. “Please tell Ms. Brown I’m here,” she told the attendant at the desk while her uniformed guards filled the dim lobby.

Kyle Foss came out to meet her with his shirt sleeves rolled up. “Thanks for doing this,” he said, smiling as he shook her hand, “I know you’ve got other places to be, but this’ll look better if you’re here in person.”

“Jim said you know your business,” Frost replied. She glanced at her watch. “I need to be in and out faster than fast.”

The multitasking manager pulled on his headset and beckoned her to follow. “We’re just going to commercials,” he explained while listening to technical chatter. “I’ve got you plugged in for two minutes. Is that quick enough?”

"I like it," Frost told him by way of compliment while they rushed down a hallway, past open doors that provided glimpses in to hectic offices. A phone in her coat pocket signaled for attention as they entered the brightly lit studio.

"Security," a man's voice boomed in her earpiece. "Hold for Richter."

Raven peeled off her parka and kept the phone while a woman stepped in close to apply makeup. "Takes off the shine under those lights," she assured.

The administrator waited silently while people came and went around her. The cosmetics expert tugged at her suit coat after finishing with face powder. "And there you go," she commented positively before moving on.

"Fifty seconds," Kyle warned while touching her on the shoulder. "Just walk on when you're ready."

Raven looked at the phone in her hand.

"It's Billy," he said out of breath. "I'm at what's left of deep data storage. We've got two lurkers. One with a thermal imager."

"Hit or miss?" Frost wanted to know.

"Direct hit," Richter pronounced after a deep breath, "As in 'X' marks the spot. They knew right where it was. Exactly. Know what I'm saying?"

"Any more tourists?" she asked while Kyle gestured for her to hurry.

"Still in motion," Billy explained.

"Go get 'em," Frost encouraged and hung up.

Kyle pointed at the moving T.V. cameras that circled Beatrice Brown. "Ten seconds," he prodded.

Raven turned off her phone and handed it to a waiting assistant. "Two minutes, Mr. Foss. I have places to go and things to do."

"One hundred and twenty seconds," the producer promised while attaching a wireless microphone to the administrator's coat lapel.

"Have a seat," Beatrice motioned as somebody rushed a small stool into place.

Frost hurried onto the set, perching on the chair as a nearby clock counted down the final seconds before air time. "How's it going?"

"Beats working," Brown joked while glamming for the nearest camera that flashed a green light.

Kyle faded into the shadows as the overhead lighting dimmed.

"Our coverage of this early morning attack of the Kodiak Starport continues with a few remarks from Senior Administrator Raven Frost," Brown summarized. "How are you holding up in the aftermath of what just happened?"

Raven projected more confidence than she felt. "I'm fine. My staff and department heads were unharmed. We're still getting a handle on the situation, so I can't say for sure what the full extent of the damage really is."

"You don't know how bad things are?"

Frost bowed her head in a gesture intended to convey remorse. "It's obviously bad. They hurt us. Lives were lost. Anyone watching our live camera feeds can see that. Let's just be thankful we didn't end up like Tokyo."

Beatrice turned in her chair to more directly address her guest. "Look to your left and you'll see what's coming through on my social media. That's one of many questions our audience would like the answers to. Why didn't we get the Tokyo treatment and what are you going to do next?"

Mindful that her two minute interval was coming to an end, Raven made eye contact with Beatrice as if they were alone. It was theater for the cameras and they both knew it. "Your guess is as good as mine," she seemed to confide. "Let the historians sort it out. We've got every resource at our disposal out there in the dark and cold, doing what they can to save lives. Whatever happens in response to this unprovoked attack will be carefully considered."

* * *

Injured men, women, and children arrived at hospitals and clinics all over Kodiak Island under the watchful eyes of freelance journalists. Audio, video, and text flowed freely, telling the stories of individuals and families harmed by an expanding war.

Some contract newshounds worked their way inside the starport perimeter to evade security patrols in an effort to capture images of military activity. By order of Billy Richter, a chosen few observed remotely and were allowed to photograph Norman Ahgupuk's F-15s as they landed. All other sensationalist shutterbugs were caught and handed over to the Alaska State Troopers before they could see anything sensitive.

"I have six bad guys in custody who are willing to talk," he told Raven by secured radio. He was sitting in his SUV, which was parked near the burning rocket fuel plant. "All of them are recent transplants with no meaningful connections to any of the major players."

"Freelance all the way?" Frost conjectured through her earpiece while shrugging into a parka in the television studio's lobby.

Billy glanced through his windshield at a passing fireman. "That's how I would've done it. Siggs and his lieutenants probably told them where we hide the good silver, but they wouldn't allow their own people to participate in anything that could be traced back to them. You know the type. People who look through a camera and send what they see without knowing a lot about what they just did."

Raven zipped up her coat as she walked out the door flanked by uninformed guards. "That means they won't know specifically who paid them, either. How long to backtrack their money trail?"

"Weeks or months," Billy replied, leaning over to see his dashboard clock. "All we can charge them with is unlawful trespass. The State Troopers might gig 'em for a few other little things, just because all of them have priors. Nothing too serious, but just enough to make any judge unhappy to see them."

Frost got into her SUV. "Hand them over and be done with it," she decided as a guard shut her door.

"When does the wind blow?"

"Soon." She reached for her seatbelt.

"As of now, all tunnels and runways are under observation," Billy said, reading from a tablet computer. "Random patrols keep everyone on their toes. North, south, east, and west are as secure as we can make them."

"Wrap up what you're doing," Raven insisted as her convoy started to move. "Be there when it happens. See everything for yourself. It's been rehearsed a hundred times. Call me if anything is out of place."

Richter signed off and got out of his vehicle. Local weather reacted to the industrial fire that was consuming the five-acre hydrogen cracking plant by making fine, gritty hail coalesce and fall with droplets of rain. Ice gathered on his SUV as Billy went to find a subordinate.

Chapter Twelve

Military and civilian helicopters began to arrive at hospitals in Anchorage that were already overloaded with patients from the catastrophe overtaking the central part of the beleaguered port city. Crisis managers worked with air traffic controllers at the Ted Stevens International Airport to begin rerouting flights to treatment facilities on the Kenai Peninsula and in the Mat-Su Valley. Clinics that could take helicopters in those regions volunteered their services.

Fires in downtown Anchorage began to spread from the fallen wreckage of the Shadow Fusion Tower as local clocks ticked past 3 a.m. Surrounding structures burned faster as combustion was forced underground, into basements and utility corridors filled with synthetic materials that were never designed to resist ignition. Police officers with flashlights blocked intersections with their cars as they began to expand the zone of evacuation.

Reporters from statewide television stations were forced away from the epicenter of destruction while firefighters looked for new ways to bring the worsening conflagration under control. Representatives from the mayor's office asked for air time on local radio stations to assure city residents that first responders had the situation under control. Some of what they said was picked up by national networks and repackaged as sound bites heard around the world.

* * *

Raven Frost approached the last checkpoint before entering the underground operations center. She flashed the ID pinned to her lapel. The armed guard nodded at her from behind a bullet-resistant panel.

Her entourage followed in a long line down the cool cement corridor. Boots and shoes squeaked on the wet floor. Raven paused to take off her parka and give it to a waiting secretary. "I want a full accounting," she demanded while smoothing wrinkles out of her clothing. "Who's alive and who's dead. Deputies and assistants will be on the job before I have breakfast."

"That's not possible for the rocket fuel plant," somebody informed her from the back of the line. "They only work a night shift and they're…gone."

The starport boss appeared unfazed as she ran her fingers through her hair. "Morning briefing will happen as normal. Call HR when they open and start hiring if there are no survivors. Work from the backlog of applications they have on file to find replacements. If anyone asks, we are still open for business."

Raven was busy on her dais in the red-lit operations area when another call came in from Raphe Chandler in aerospace operations. "Five minutes," he advised.

"Move to first position."

Frost had just started a conference call with the starport's fire chief when she received a priority signal on a seldom used hotline. The encrypted phone buzzed for attention as she excused herself. "Sorry," she apologized to the emergency services manager. "You've got your fires to put out and, unfortunately, I've got mine."

Identification codes displayed on the sleek, red, modern handset indicated that the scrambled call was coming from the Jiuquan Starport, deep inside mainland China. "Kodiak Starport," Raven answered after typing in her activation code. "This is Administrator Frost. I hope we haven't been keeping you up too late."

"Please hold for Administrator Andrew Lao," a female voice requested.

"Certainly," Frost consented, texting her electronic intelligence unit to monitor the call.

A series of chirps preceded Administrator Lao's voice. "Good morning," he started, speaking English with a Mandarin accent. "I'm so glad we can speak directly."

"Indeed."

"Please let me get to the point," he continued courteously. "You have lost your basic space launch capability. Launch, recovery, electricity generation, and propellants production have all been handicapped. Nothing more than you would need to reach low orbit with a meaningful payload. All other facilities are still intact. You'll be profitable again within two calendar years, if we allow it."

"That's one way of looking at it."

Andrew proceeded without acknowledging her wit. "Your predecessor was given a chance to stand down, with compensation. You've now been forced to do so without benefits. As long as we understand each other, I see no need to apply any further pressure. It's not our war. Let's put our differences aside and—"

"No."

"Excuse me?" he paused calmly.

Frost took a deep breath and let it out. "It is my war now," she asserted precisely. "You've seen to that. If Jim was here, he'd have a few more words for you that I'm not comfortable with using, but I promise, you're about to hear what we have to say, loud and clear!"

"Threats are meaningless," Lao countered. "Your corporate leadership has been decapitated and whatever you're thinking of won't work. That includes your space planes," he revealed slyly. "We've known about them for six months. I assure you that our air defenses are far more integrated than the hodgepodge you relied on."

Raven's stomach churned and her heart fluttered. "You sound pretty sure of yourself," she stalled while her mind raced.

"I am," Andrew snapped.

Text messages from the Baikonur Starport came to Frost's attention as they scrolled across the central display on her dais through an encrypted channel. *Administrator Kalugen sends regards. Regret to inform you that all major facilities are offline for unscheduled holiday maintenance. We apologize for this inconvenience.* Russian aerospace officials must've been weighing their options ever since news of the Tokyo incident came to their attention. This unofficial notification was their way of giving her a free hand without obligating anyone in Moscow to say or do anything they might regret.

"Well, then," she snickered while she composed a response to Baikonur. "I wouldn't want to keep you waiting."

"What is that supposed to mean?"

Kodiak requests trans-polar path through Siberian air defense corridor, she typed. "Find your secretary, Mr. Lao," Raven said smugly. "I can never seem to locate mine. You're going to need one before this is over."

All radars down for repairs, Baikonur replied. *Wouldn't see Santa if he came through.*

"What are you talking about?"

"Resignation letter," Raven clarified. "You'll want somebody to help you with that when this is all over."

"You have one hour to reconsider—" Lao erupted.

Thank you, she wrote to Baikonur.

"Don't need it," she shot back at Andrew before hanging up on him. Sitting back in her chair, she called the aerospace controller.

"What's the word?" Chandler asked over the roar of scramjets.

"Launch when ready."

* * *

Still photos and camera feeds used to enhance Beatrice Brown's broadcast changed as she spoke. Preselected video loops were incorporated into her ongoing narration to hide what observers on the ground may have seen in the predawn twilight.

Sirens wailed across the starport. "Air defense warning!" a now-familiar automated voice warned through loudspeakers. "This is not a drill. All employees, report to your duty stations. Civilians, please go to the nearest emergency accommodation."

Below ground in fortified corridors, each of the starport's four aerospace fighters rested on rocket-assisted catapults. Their long, flat, teardrop shapes were bathed in bright light that made it easier for retreating technicians to look for loose tools and equipment. The men and women walked out of each chamber or climbed ladder assemblies to leave through dimly lit ventilation conduits that would take them back to workshops and office spaces where they could view what happened next in safety.

Flight systems engineers in nearby bunkers communicated with pilots through encrypted. Digital data uplinks sent information to and received it from dozens of computers in each space plane.

"Begin sequence," the lead flight controller ordered, starting an old fashioned stopwatch that hung on a lanyard around t neck.

"North wind engaging catapult," the designated flight leader reported from his cockpit.

"South wind is go," the next pilot replied.

"East wind go," number three called out with a jolt.

"West wind is hot," the last voice chimed in.

Located four geographic miles apart, each space plane was flung down the length of its own underground runway on a rocket sled. They separated from their speeding trollies as each aerodynamic lifting body accelerated through the sound barrier. Scramjets thundered to life as the aerospace fighters emerged into the open at 3,000 miles per hour within half a second of each other. Racing into the predawn sky on tails of flame, they shed their booster rockets after an undulating two-minute burn that jarred each pilot into momentary unconsciousness.

Few of the civilians or first responders who were out in the open paid attention to that spectacle. Those who happened to be looking in the right direction had very little time to photograph vanishing lights. Sonic booms that a vocal minority claimed to hear were drowned out by the racket of industrial fires continuing to advance across the starport, in spite of heroic efforts to stop them.

* * *

Beatrice Brown frowned as she read from the nearest teleprompter. "Residents in the civilian employee housing sector are advised to begin packing for evacuation. Fires at the rocket fuel plant that was hit earlier tonight are getting out of control. Several blazes have merged. Two are spreading towards Boom Town."

She paused to maintain her composure while a camera roamed in close. "It's been a long night for all of us. I wish we had better news, but you're seeing this as it is happening. As you may recall from my conversation with this starport's fire chief, our resources are stretched to their limit. The new administrator, Raven Frost, assures me that we'll get a break soon. Some sort of lull that will allow everyone to get a handle on the situation."

* * *

Andre Allison looked over his shoulder at Raven, pointing at the nearest big screen that projected the starport news. "That woman could sell water to a whale," he said, smiling.

"I'll keep that in mind," Frost murmured while holding out a computer tablet with one hand. "Here. Take this. Norman is on the ground and his section leaders are refueling. They'll rejoin their combat air patrols to fly in shifts. We've lost parts of our network, so I want you to do this by hand."

The launch coordinator came closer. Emergency lighting didn't darken his mood. "Nanook is up and gone," he chatted while grabbing the device and reading from its small screen. "News feeds are being restored to live shots of the smoke and fire. Speaking of which, that was quite the spicy confab with Jiuquan. Have you ever met Andy Lao?"

"No."

"Nice guy," Andre recalled while going through pages of instructions.

"Remember that if you ever have my job."

CHAPTER THIRTEEN

Pentagon representatives in Washington D.C. released written remarks to the media rather than appear on camera to comment on the implications of the attack. Many of these press releases contained same or similar phrasing. A very brief statement from the Chairs of the House and Senate Armed Services Committees read in part, "The crisis at the Kodiak Starport is being carefully monitored. All options are being considered."

An interservice team comprised of high ranking officers from the Joint Chiefs of Staff met with senior White House policy advisors to draft a list of recommendations for review by the Commander in Chief. Unnamed sources leaked vaguely worded extracts to the media that suggested the Administration might initiate a strong U.S. naval response in reaction to the attacks that had crippled the Kodiak Starport.

Reaction to the time-honored "trial balloon" was mixed. Pro-American media outlets speculated on the nature of U.S. naval activity, to include openly guessing which carrier battlegroups, submarines, and warships might be called on for such dangerous duty, based on their last publicly known locations. Friendly governments made noncommittal statements that could be bolstered or taken back later, depending on the outcome of early battles. Hostile regimes proclaimed victory through every form of communication.

Astute commentators and social media personalities perceived meaning in Beatrice Brown's presentation, going so far as to hypothesize about what she really meant. Conspiracy theorists offered the most sensational interpretations of her reportage.

"Have you noticed that what she says doesn't always match up with the video?"

"That sounds like a hint. What does Frost mean by a 'break' or a 'lull?'"

"I'm telling you, Sasha Xavier has a hand in this. I just know it!"

* * *

Norman Ahgupuk walked into the underground operations center wearing his flightsuit and insulated boots to see a plot of the starport's airspace projected on several of the largest overhead screens. He flagged down a passing beverage cart to ask the attendant for a paper cup filled with coffee as he listened to radio traffic.

"Gatekeeper turning inbound," the 747's pilot informed ground-based controllers.

A senior air traffic specialist made corrections to the formation as it approached Kodiak Island. "Sentry Flight, increase your interval to five miles."

"Roger," Captain Hancock acknowledged in his role as leader.

Norman sauntered slowly toward the center of the room while his vision adjusted to the soft red glow. He sipped coffee at the bottom of the dais while waiting for the busy starport boss to speak with him. Shifting images on dozens of screens and holographic projections allowed him to passively catch up on recent events. Interviews and viewer call-ins conducted over the last few frantic hours were being recapped with extensive commercial breaks. It wasn't hard for him to imagine the exhausted journalist collapsed on a couch somewhere, sleeping deeply, while Kyle Foss and his army of producers and technicians kept the world watching.

"Negative horizon sweep," Gatekeeper reported through static.

Ahgupuk turned to see Raven Frost standing behind him. "Quiet when you want to be," he observed through his fatigue. "Can I assume they're talking about—"

"No, you can't," she interrupted from the bottom step.

He opened a pocket and took out a slim computer. "Networks are down at the airfield," he explained, handing it to her. "I sent this to the intell unit, but I thought you'd want to see it."

"What have we got?" Raven asked as she took the tablet and held it close.

Norman shrugged. "Everything Gatekeeper saw. The little bit our gun cameras got a look at. Audio, video, sensor tracks. The whole nine yards."

"What do you make of it?"

The pilot scratched stubble on his chin. "I want one," he confessed.

"Are they that good?"

"Anyone who tells you they aren't is lying," he assessed uncomfortably. "Tactics change. We'll never be able to whack 'em like that again."

Frost made eye contact. "Could they do that to us?"

"Yes." Ahgupuk gestured with his coffee cup while he talked. "There's enough descending debris in the low orbit pathways right now to prevent anyone from staying up there for very long. Problem is getting conventional jets up there long enough to make an intercept. It's almost like basketball, and hang time at the net when you want to block—"

"I get it," Raven waved him off with one hand.

Norman finished his coffee and threw the empty cup away in a nearby trash can. "Basketball is a team sport," he coughed. "I didn't play by your rules."

"Don't apologize for being right."

"A lot of air forces have trained for this," he clarified. "We got lucky. We have a few pilots that went through those programs. As unlikely as this situation was, we had to use—"

"You've made your point."

"You've got my report." The combat veteran glanced over his shoulder. "Everybody with wings has a job to do, except me. How can I help?"

The administrator tapped her watch. "I'm going to break a few rules in the next hour and a half. It would make me feel better if you were in the air defense bunker, just in case."

Norman laughed while turning to leave. "We'll keep the skies clear for whatever you have in mind."

* * *

"Which is what, exactly?" Air Force Major General Xiao Lung demanded.

"The same thing we did to them!" Senior Administrator Andrew Lao insisted in Mandarin through the secure telephone line connected to an undisclosed location somewhere in Gensu province. "She all but threatened me with it, in so many words," he ranted.

Xiao was unimpressed. "Don't you think we planned for this? There are two squadrons equipped with anti-satellite missiles on rotation over your head right now. Andrew, get a grip on your situation. Nothing has been left to chance. There isn't anything they can do to you that we haven't considered. That includes a low orbit attack—if they are capable of it!"

Lao was a party-approved executive with many political connections and every leadership credential needed to manage a large workforce. Limited military service in noncombat assignments and a lack of experience in the fields of aviation and spaceflight amplified his concerns. Acting on orders from Beijing to unleash an aerospace attack was one thing. Based on what he'd seen of news reports from Japan and Alaska, surviving a similar event would be something else entirely.

According to published sources, Raven Frost's background indicated a lack of corporate political ambition, though she displayed superior skill at crisis management that earned her a reputation for being quick to adapt in stressful situations. Military and intelligence analysts added notations that suggested a knack for delegation. These traits made Lao think she was willing to order an attack on his starport if she could retaliate.

"I would if I could," he mumbled to the black plastic handset while looking around his large well-appointed office. He continued speaking at a more normal volume. "General, she doesn't have many good options. In her place, I would answer this with a similar mission. Based on the rather indiscreet inquiry they've made through the underworld, I think they intend to—"

"Administrator Lao," General Lung interrupted, "your concerns have been duly noted. If there is more to be done, it will, I assure you, be taken care of by people in a position to make those decisions!"

* * *

All four aerospace fighters from Kodiak reached their desired cruising altitude without any mishaps, despite the rising smoke and debris emanating from the structure fires inside the starport's well-marked and brightly lit perimeter. The lack of operational satellites in low orbit allowed all four space planes to fly unobserved through Russian airspace on a trajectory that took them out over the Arctic Ocean.

Ground based military radars, lidars, and thermal detection systems registered the atmospheric disturbances that the supersonic ships made when passing through the Siberian air defenses. Acting on orders from Moscow, regional commanders kept their missile batteries on standby. Conventional jet fighter squadrons that could've attempted to intercept them were inexplicably grounded.

Few pieces of falling debris hit the space planes as they remained inside the Earth's thin atmosphere. Jettisoning the first of their spent fuel tanks as they reached apogee, the pilots were kept busy with engine operation calculations and course changes while talking through encrypted channels.

"Top of the world," North Wind reported to Kodiak controllers. "Thirty seconds 'til loss of reception. Go or no go?"

Raven's voice filled his helmet. "Administrator One-One authorizes full go."

The flight leader opened a paper notebook strapped to his thigh and glanced at a page filled with columns of letters and numbers. "Authenticate," he requested.

Frost quickly read out a sequence.

"Mission is full go," he confirmed when the sequence matched an entry circled in red.

"Good luck and good hunting."

* * *

Worldwide audiences viewing multimedia streams from the Kodiak Starport began to include intelligence analysts. Government war planners studied what they saw with growing interest as Beatrice Brown reported on the worsening fires that consumed more above ground structures at the Alaskan space launch complex. Civilian logisticians observed each segment between commercials with their own priorities in mind.

Social media buzzed with lurid dissections of the catastrophes in downtown Tokyo and on Kodiak Island. The difference in coverage was stark. Japanese news anchors were more formal and less specific as they came and went in teams throughout the night. Kodiak

Starport's one and only commentator showed signs of fatigue before being replaced by produced segments that rehashed the most recent tragedies.

Conspiracy theorists complained about what they didn't see. American commentators made the most of what was presented, to include sensationalizing acts of heroism that occasionally appeared on-camera when firefighters or paramedics rescued civilian workers from harrowing circumstances.

Media personalities from hostile nations chose less flattering instances to replay that did include the loss of life. These misfortunes were solemnly discussed by panels of soft spoken experts, or disparaged by brazen comedians in ways that were intended to be humorous.

High ranking officials in Beijing, who had time to see broadcasts from Alaska and Japan, drew their own conclusions while receiving updated intelligence reports from those locales.

Damage assessments indicated that Tokyo starport was a total loss, with an increasing death toll. Ongoing audio and video traffic suggested that Kodiak Starport security services prevented many prepaid observers from getting a good look at the targets that had been hit during the aerospace attack. As bad as Beatrice Brown made it look and sound, they had no way of knowing just how damaged the Alaskan facility really was.

Administrator Lao's conversation with Major General Xiao Lung was transformed in to a three-page document that found its way into the flow of information that informed and influenced these leaders. One after another, departments added corroborating assessments to the starport administrator's concern over a possible enemy aerospace attack, until the addendum contained 73 pages of sensitive or secret material. The enlarged report was redefined as a high priority case study and resubmitted to the country's top intelligence officials for immediate consideration.

* * *

Emergency meetings were called to consult with national and theater aerospace defense coordinators, who briefed Communist party advisors. A timeline of the attacks on the starports in Tokyo and Kodiak were examined. Jiuquan Starport's air defense plan was explained, when arguments broke out over contingency plans.

Administrator Lao and his senior staff were consulted by secure telephone when clarifications were needed. Acting on up-to-date information, defense and intelligence experts agreed that Jiuquan Starport was at risk. Working with an approved list of available resources, that hastily assembled working group formulated a detailed description of options. These were presented to the Central Committee's go-betweens, who anxiously awaited the new document while they watched two different starports burn on separate infotainment channels.

Chapter Fourteen

Raven waved at the launch coordinator. "Mr. Allison, it's coming up on 4 a.m. Set area lighting to normal. We might as well get ready for the day shift."

"Morning brief in two hours," Andre said through a yawn while walking by the dais. His fatigue spread like a contagion through the workforce, which made some people pause to laugh as they tried to shake it off.

She blinked and exhaled sympathetically as the overhead lighting slowly changed from red to white. She rubbed her aching ear to adjust the device that was clipped to it. "Call Richter," she told her phone, sipping cold coffee from a blue mug to hide a smile.

"Sorry I didn't get back to you," Billy apologized when he picked up.

Frost quickly typed orders for another department while she talked. "Fire chief needs help. Lend him all the warm bodies you can spare. Draft civilians you know and trust, while you're at it. Do a slow roll through Boom Town and make sure the holdouts know how serious the situation is."

"That's what held me up," he complained. "I've got everyone on the payroll out here directing traffic, watching the exits, or applying first aid. We can ignore minor looting, but eventually—"

"I know!"

Billy paused for several seconds. "My people are working with the State Troopers to formally charge some of the people we've rounded up. That ought to keep the insurance adjusters happy."

"Thanks."

"I thought you'd like to hear it from me before blabbermouth makes a big deal out of it," Richter joked.

"She's just doing her job."

Billy laughed. "Anyone who sees this mess on television—"

"We do have this under control," Frost reprimanded.

"Yes ma'am," he replied with some contrition.

"Call me while you're in Boom Town," she asked. "I want to know what it looks like before fire crews have to go in there."

"Will do," he confirmed before signing off.

* * *

American war planners were made aware of a subtle shift in the opposition's domestic air defense strategy when U.S. Navy drones and manned reconnaissance aircraft that were flying at very high altitudes in Japanese airspace detected squadron-level movements in eastern mainland China. Decoded message traffic indicated some urgency in the reallocation. This baffled Pentagon analysts because they couldn't identify any natural or manmade threats to those regions, nor were they aware of any ongoing missions in those provinces that may have been discovered to be 'in progress.'

U.S. and allied intelligence resources inside China were slow to respond when asked about squadron dispositions. Complaints from far-flung provinces tasked with providing increased air cover for all parts of eastern China were copied and sent to Washington.

Deep cover agents revealed that specialized detachments of modified all-weather, multi-role fighters were being relocated from secured sites near Beijing to military airfields next to Jiuquan Starport.

* * *

"Something is happening that we're not aware of," a presidential advisory team concluded in Washington D.C. "Somebody has guessed Kodiak's next move, and they're gearing up to take the punch. If so, this represents an escalation that may be unmanageable."

Recent sensor activity from remote stations on the Kenai Peninsula, near Homer, was still being examined by multiple defense and intelligence agencies when new questions were raised about the situation on Kodiak Island by executive branch thinkers. "Have they responded with Nanook?" they wanted to know.

Sixty vital minutes passed before meaningful answers trickled in. There was no conclusive evidence of an aerospace response from Kodiak, nor was there any reference to a reprisal in the starport's ongoing media presentation. North American Aerospace Defense Command installations in Alaska and Canada reviewed their recorded data. Technicians put on cold weather gear and boarded VTOLs with tools and spare parts. They were flown out to remote locations to report firsthand on the condition of antennas, transmitters, and receivers as quickly as possible.

* * *

Alaska's theater commander, U.S. Army Lieutenant General Manika Sachdeva, observed the unfolding military situation far below ground somewhere on Joint Base Wainwright-Eielson. Displays and instrument readouts of all sorts around the dimly lit combat information center could easily be seen from inside her enclosed office, where she sat drinking fresh coffee from a mug with the 25th Infantry Division's logo on it. Transparent walls kept out sound as she watched uniformed men and women come and go from a variety of workstations.

The four-story administrative bunker was more than a command and control facility filled with enough food, water, and medical supplies to keep a hundred and fifty people insulated from the cold for six months. Every level and entry point was protected against nuclear and biochemical threats. Whatever the place lacked in comfort, it made up for in survivability.

"Opinions are forming," she told Raven through a secured phone connection. "Sensor tracks do indicate activity. No more than we anticipated. That means my superiors will be asking about Nanook any time now."

"Have they got real proof or are they guessing?" Frost inquired procedurally from the privacy of her office overlooking the starport's much larger operations area.

The general was alone. She put her cup down and looked at the phone while gathering her thoughts. "Wouldn't matter if they knew, or if they were spitting in the wind. They ask and I answer. That's how it works."

"It's only going to matter when they send you to conduct the first round of inquiries."

Manika glanced at her own desktop chronometer. "True. And…I'm sorry about Jim. Things have been moving so fast, there hasn't been time for condolences. How are you holding up?"

Raven looked around her shadow-filled office. "I'm all right. First strike hits in about 30 minutes, give or take. I have it on good authority that Governor Wheeler is already stonewalling for us. Any breathing room you can give us will be appreciated."

"Consider it done."

* * *

Beatrice Brown stepped out into the cluttered hallway and closed the door to her dark office. "Whose bright idea was it to let me sleep so long?"

"My decision," Kyle Foss told her from the shadows.

"Are you a cruise director now?" She frowned while pulling wrinkles out of her clothing.

He laughed as he loosened his necktie. "You were snoring and our ratings are flying high. I got a call from upstairs a few minutes ago. They have something big in the works that'll need your attention. So, here I am."

"Special treatment?"

"First class." Kyle genuflected. "We have early breakfast service in the lounge, just in case you'd like to have a bite before we go back."

"Just send somebody for me next time."

The station manager walked with her, weaving around equipment trollies. "You're not the only one who likes to get away from that circus."

"Any idea what the big surprise is?"

"Not a clue," he confessed, holding a door open. "I was told to expect prepared text. That could mean just about anything."

Brown walked into the furnished room, where she took a plate from a catering cart and waited in line behind other people to get some hot food. "Sounds like trouble for somebody," she whispered over her shoulder. "You did say the ratings are good?"

"Sky high," Foss bragged.

* * *

Acting on orders that came to them through high priority channels, coastal theater Air Force commands in Shanghai and Hong Kong released their special duty air defense squadrons. The handoff to Jiuquan province was easy enough for senior air traffic controllers to comply with, though several wondered why the request was so urgent.

"What's this about?" one of them asked a colleague at Jiuquan Starport.

"Tokyo," their source responded dryly.

Gossip quickly spread through social media, crossing over into secure voice communications between departments. Somebody claiming to know something about a classified report to or from the Central Committee related to a possible aerospace attack supposed that it was connected to the Jiuquan Starport. That one off-the-cuff speculation, later alleged to have come from a supposedly credible source that nobody could locate, added to an increasing sense of anxiety that crept through leadership circles.

* * *

"Say that again?" Billy shouted into his radio as an ambulance roared by.

"Contained!" the fire chief came back through interference, "Holding. As long as the water pressure doesn't give out, we've got it contained! I can release two of your men from traffic duty, if you want 'em."

Richter brushed soot off his parka and leaned on the ice-covered door of his SUV, watching the glowing Boom Town skyline shimmer for several seconds while nearby paramedics packed to leave. He'd been rushing from one fire zone to the next for the last 40 minutes in an effort to reallocate his workforce as casualties took their toll. "I can still see major concentrations," he reported using a handheld microphone. "North to south, looks like all of the low rent housing is gone."

"Not as bad as it looks," the senior firefighter insisted. "Fifty percent, no more. Better tell the boss there has been some loss. No idea how many, but we've already found a few civvies. There will be more."

"What else can you tell me about the looting?" Billy asked, reaching into his vehicle for a tablet computer.

"Get over here and do something about it!"

* * *

Norman Ahgupuk drank deeply from the mug of strong coffee offered to him by one of the radar technicians seated nearby. "Oh! Ack! That's a war crime!" he cursed while chugging the bitter brew, "Hit me again—just half," he reconsidered while returning the empty cup.

Gobbling down half a sandwich in three bites, Norman turned in his chair to see what was going on around him. Bread crumbs fell as he watched people work and listened to radio chatter. A phone interrupted his moment with an insistent warble.

"Air defense," he answered with his mouth full.

"Sounds more like the cafeteria," Raven teased. "It's just on 4:45. What's the situation with your airplanes?"

"Don't you have—"

"I'm asking you," she pressed.

"Well," Norman replied, wiping his mouth, "We have three shifts of six birds, one up and two down. Alert group is on the apron for immediate takeoff. The rest are in the shop for maintenance."

"Morale?"

"Positive," he nodded while gripping the handset. "Great, actually. It's a little hard to believe we got one. What's this all about?"

"Make sure everything is in good order and then go to the television studio," Raven told him. "Get a shower and a something like a clean uniform. Be there in 25 minutes, no later."

"Again, I ask. What's going on?"

"Remember what you got for Christmas?" Frost enunciated delicately.

"Yes…"

"Time to open presents," she suggested craftily. "They'll need some commentary from a credible source. Somebody who might be able to make something of what they're looking at, as it happens."

"Now?"

"Please hurry, you've only got 24 minutes."

CHAPTER FIFTEEN

The Kodiak formation reached the edge of space, releasing the last of their spent external fuel tanks as all four ships spread out inside the Earth's thin atmosphere, well below the danger zone of descending wreckage. There were no manned aircraft or remotely controlled observers loitering at high altitude to detect the formation. This allowed all four space planes to fly through Russian and American airspace without being optically "seen" as they circled the Earth, heading south toward the bottom of the world.

* * *

U.S. intelligence analysts were intrigued by an unexplained lack of Russian ground radar activity while they were examining sporadic contacts that did appear to originate from Kodiak Island.

"Somebody is leaving the game open," they concluded.

Presidential advisors in Washington D.C. discussed the implications of Kodiak Starport's apparent response and what it could mean for U.S. foreign policy before meeting with the Commander in Chief shortly after 9 a.m. Eastern Time.

The Air Force representative summarized their understanding of the situation. "Looks like an aerospace attack. Their target appears to be Jiuquan. Tit for tat, same as they got. That means multiple kinetic strikes."

"What are the Chinese doing?" the Chief of Staff asked.

"As you'd expect," the general indicated as he handed updated reports to his counterparts, "their starport is on alert and the skies are full. That place is inland, so they need to rely on high altitude fighters to get missiles in position. Thing is, they can do it. Lots of them!"

"We need a response," the State Department advisor warned, pointing at his gold wristwatch. "Mr. President, you gave Kodiak a free hand and they used it. That means we react to whatever this is. Wait and see what happens, then you speak—after an appropriate period of consultation with diplomats and national leaders, which is what your press secretary says to the media when they ask."

* * *

Plunging southward towards Antarctica, all four pilots marveled at the vast expanse that passed below them. Small pieces of falling debris from destroyed platforms struck the Kodiak aerospace fighters, slowly degrading the effectiveness of their radar-reflective coatings. This slow loss of their stealth capability was minimized by the gradually descending flight path of the strike force as it zoomed over the Antarctic Ocean, between Australia and New Zealand, and above the South Pacific Ocean at extreme speed.

Spy satellites in high orbit caught momentary glimpses of the fast moving vehicles and their heat trails. Uncertain observations were reclassified as 'accurate' once new sightings were verified. Lengthy observations poured in, proving conclusively that four aerospace vehicles from Kodiak were transiting the central Pacific Ocean on trajectories bound for Chinese airspace.

* * *

"I told you so—she's just that direct!" Andrew Lao boasted through his headset microphone over a secured land line. It was just after 10 p.m. The connection was being made over a secured landline to a nearby air force base. Crimson area lighting permeated his underground operations area with a tense atmosphere. Men and women in color coded uniforms came and went from workstations arranged in a crescent pattern that allowed the amphitheater-style chamber to make the most of its acoustics.

A difference of 16 hours between Alaska and mainland China meant that it was already evening of the next calendar day when Major General Xiao Lung glanced through his office window to see jets moving up and down a network of lighted runways.

"Have your ships landed?" he asked while bending over his desk to work with a computer.

The administrator looked at his own status boards out of habit. "They're coming in now. Final approach in six minutes."

The senior officer stood up to ease the pain in his back while he read from the screen on his desk. Jet engines roared on the flight line, shaking all of the furniture in his office. Pictures rattled on the walls.

"Losses?"

"As projected," Andrew prefaced, "just one, from an ASM."

"Airborne or surface launch?" the general inquired.

"Airborne." Lao added, "General, my people are telling me that the inbound strike force is accelerating. They'll be here before we can get our ships refueled and rearmed. Is there any chance the Navy can intercept them while they are still at sea?"

Xiao chuckled at the thought. "Administrator, there isn't a carrier-based airplane on this planet that could catch them. Not now."

The senior executive eyed a shimmering air defense plot that was projected on the ceiling over his head. "Very well, then. Luck is with us. Our squadrons will begin their climb to best altitude when the time comes, to destroy them when they get here."

General Lung walked around his desk to get a better look at the nighttime airfield. A lack of moisture in the air kept ice from forming on the ground as local temperatures remained below freezing. "Refuel and rearm your ships when they land. Activate the reserve fighters and have them go with the next sortie."

"What about—"

"No more interference from bureaucrats!" Xiao barked. "Do it quickly, before Beijing gets involved! How soon can you be ready?"

The starport boss referred to the tablet computer in his hand. "No more than two hours," he determined after flicking through a few menus. "There will be some delay, just because we'll need to—"

"Don't bother me with details!"

"I will be happy to follow your orders when I get them," Andrew responded obsequiously. "Tomorrow morning, Kodiak starport will be out of business."

* * *

Flying a course that took them over occupied Malaysia, the Kodiak strike force approached the South China Sea. Ground based radars and intelligence gathering posts in the region caught sight of the four space planes as they passed overhead at hypersonic speed, in spite of their extreme altitude in the night sky. Optical and thermal images were transmitted to Chinese military analysts who compared that information with what they were getting from spy satellites in high orbit. Reassured by their findings, they began to estimate possible destinations for the inbound attack.

* * *

Anticipation spread through the Jiuquan operations amphitheater when the Kodiak aerospace attack formation appeared on the national air defense projection as a bright blue pulsating dot, labeled K-1. Heads turned to glance furtively at the rapidly moving track. Gossip started slowly while live programming from approved networks streamed on screens around the chamber.

"They want us to see them coming," somebody whispered from a nearby workstation.

"Of course they do," Administrator Lao reproached the unseen speaker from the chair attached to his elevated podium. "You know how much of a preening showman their last administrator was! We have the upper hand," he declared with a sweeping gesture. "Our fighters are waiting to blow them out of the sky!"

A buzzing telephone was answered by Lao's personal assistant. She addressed him from her desk behind his elevated position. "The media department has selected a commentator to broadcast reaction to the attack. They were impressed with Kodiak's presentation, so they thought you might want live coverage of the event."

"No." Andrew rounded on her by swiveling his chair. "Absolutely not! Not one word of this gets out until that Alaskan circus has been dealt with. A little patience and a few carefully chosen words after the fact will be good for all of us."

The operations officer stepped into view. "Combat air patrols are at their assigned radius. I'd like to raise our alert level, so we can clear the roads for military use."

"Do it!" Lao commanded confidently. "Bring the complex to maximum alert and activate the air defenses, all batteries. Time the civilian evacuation. I want to know how long it takes to reach shelter capacity. What is the estimated time of attack?"

"Twenty minutes," a specialist called out.

* * *

Billy Richter rushed into the television studio, followed by two armed guards in cold weather gear. He paused to stomp mud and slush off his recently polished boots while his protectors took off their parkas.

"You cleaned up nicely," Beatrice Brown remarked from a warm corner of the lobby.

Richter scratched his head with a free hand. "Fastest haircut in the north," he laughed while tearing open his coat to reveal a new uniform, complete with patches and insignia.

"Thanks for the effort," she complimented.

The starport guards hung their coats on a nearby rack and stood aside. Billy gave one of them his parka and tugged the wrinkles out of his shirt and pants.

"What's this all about?"

"We've been told to expect a major event," Brown related plainly.

"I just came from a major event," Billy grunted. "Every section of Boom Town that isn't on fire is being picked over by looters."

"It's being kept off the air," she promised.

"Really?"

Beatrice bristled. "I'm not here to make you look bad, but I am going to tell the truth—when I can!"

"Is Norman going to share in this glam fest?" he deflected.

She pointed down a dark hallway. "Any minute now. If you'll come with me, I have a few things to do before we start."

Richter nodded. "Good. I don't want all this fame just for myself."

* * *

Administrator Lao sat up when the projected plot of the inbound aerospace attack changed. Two blue dots now appeared on the national air defense board, labeled K-1 and K-2. K-1 appeared to change course and speed, moving slightly faster than K-2.

"Refresh that," he ordered without thinking.

"No mistake," the operations officer informed him from across the room as the military projection reset. "New threat assessments are being uploaded. K-1 is on course for Shanghai. K-2 is turning for Hong Kong. Estimates are still being worked out, but they look like two ship elements."

"They're not coming for us?" a nearby technician breathed in amazement.

"*No,*" Andrew muttered fearfully. "That's wrong. Somebody—anybody!" he shouted urgently from his perch. "Tell me, what's in or near those locations that would be worth all this effort?"

Voices babbled while hands reached for telephones or hammered keyboards.

"—has a regional military command post."

"What if they're going after the nuclear power stations?"

Andrew stood and looked around to get a better feel for what was happening. Rotating images on several small monitors caused him to notice the newsfeeds his secretary was watching at her desk. An ad for popular snacks faded, replaced by the smiling face of a well-known news anchor. She was talking to a photogenic admiral and a trio of cheerful pilots, all with medals on their uniformed chests.

The administrator's jaw dropped when he saw the vibrant lettering at the bottom of each screen proudly advertising that the broadcast was live from Shanghai.

* * *

Air defense managers in southcentral mainland China followed the progress of Kodiak's aerospace fighters with growing interest, comparing the optical sightings from trusted intelligence gathering ships at sea with more detailed information from their own land-based installations. Course and speed of the intruders suggested that something in or near cities of Hong Kong and Shanghai was about to be hit. A computer-generated list of targets for each location began to grow as the likelihood of attack increased.

Conventional jet fighters at a dozen coastal air bases scrambled. Soldiers and military police in Shanghai and Hong Kong were mobilized. A series of encrypted telephone calls through isolated landline systems. This allowed experienced battery commanders in those cities to confer off the record for several minutes before they agreed on recommendations that were forwarded to their superiors.

Alarms honked, hooted, and moaned throughout the concrete canyons of central Hong Kong and the massive metroplex of Shanghai. Traffic came to a standstill in urban areas as intersection lighting became unpredictable. Police, fire, and ambulance units fought for lane space with buses, delivery vans, and long lines of troop carriers, while rushing to preassigned locations. Lights turned on and off chaotically when building managers took personal initiative to aid in civil evacuations or followed military orders to begin blackouts intended to reduce enemy air raid effectiveness.

* * *

Beatrice sat in her studio chair and straightened her jacket. Billy perched on the edge of a chair to her left, while Norman sat more casually to her right. A trio of makeup technicians rushed around all three of them with open kits.

"What's that all about?"

"Monitor two, sound up!" she told the voice-activated console.

Voices and video poured out of the small display that was tuned to one of the top three Chinese infotainment networks. A calm voice delivered commentary in English with Mandarin subtitles over scenes of martial preparation.

"—air raid warnings in Shanghai and Hong Kong continue, based on what government officials are calling 'an imminent aerospace threat.' Local authorities encourage everyone to comply with emergency orders."

"That would be the major event we were told to expect," Norman supposed while a hairdresser worked him over quickly.

"You know something about this?" Billy inquired with a sidelong glance.

"Obviously," the pilot grumbled with a mixture of fatigue and sarcasm as all three makeup technicians left the stage. "Tell us to get dressed up for something we have to talk about without knowing what it is."

Beatrice put a hand on each man's shoulder. "You lucky men. Welcome to my world! See that teleprompter? Any minute now, our prerecorded material wraps and the commercial break ends. The screen lights up with all sorts of surprises."

Richter eyed the scrolling presentation. "Is that us? Are we doing that?"

* * *

Anchored off the coast of a former British colony under blackout conditions, China's newest aircraft carrier bustled with activity. *Peoples Prosperity* (*Rénmín fánróng*) was the sister ship of the late *Strong Prosperity* (*Qiángdà de shǔxìng*), which had been destroyed two years earlier by a spectacular "rail gun" attack, from the Kodiak Starport's *Gold Rush* space station.

Peoples Prosperity was more than a replacement or a manifestation of industrial power. Surrounded by capital ships that provided a wide array of capabilities to the flotilla, it had just returned from a successful deployment. State-approved media was on hand to celebrate officers and crew, who were being encouraged to tell their stories to a nation that wanted to hear about their victories.

Coverage was abruptly terminated when every ship in the battle group went to action stations. Klaxons could be heard blaring across the harbor as live camera feeds were suddenly turned off by order of government officials on land. Officers and crew on assignment ashore or on vacation inland were immediately recalled while sailors and aviators on watch went to their battle stations.

Fighters on combat air patrol from the *Peoples Prosperity* raced to their maximum altitudes, where they were joined by squadrons from coastal commands. Additional fighters were still being connected to steam-powered catapults and launched when a pair of aerospace fighters from Kodiak Starport passed directly over *Peoples Prosperity* at an altitude far beyond the reach of conventional air defense.

The two-ship formation, denoted on the Chinese national air defense plot as K-1, was miles away from the aircraft carrier before one depleted uranium rod from each plane hit and penetrated the flattop, boring through all of its decks and compartments. Each shaft disintegrated as it passed through the vessel's bottom in a spray of superheated plasma that boiled away 10,000 cubic yards of water.

That event was witnessed from dry land by independent journalists and bloggers. These observers heard a thunderclap in the darkness, followed by the sight of a luminous cloud of rising steam that hid the silhouette of *Peoples Prosperity* from view before it appeared to erupt in flames that reached for the sky. A series of rolling detonations heralded the ignition of aviation fuel and ammunition bunkers that split the stricken ship in half.

Leaders in Shanghai bunkers watched the approaching high-altitude radar track, designated K-1, with a growing sense of dread as activity reports flooded their command posts. Tense minutes passed. Audio, video, and text messages indicating force readiness did little to reassure politicians and generals, who saw illegal broadcasts from Hong Kong streamed through their unregistered personal devices.

Sirens in and around the city wailed. Live media coverage was curtailed. Air defense and automotive traffic managers seemed to have a better grip on their situations as military and civilian police units took control of city. Armed jets and helicopters filled the night sky at prearranged altitudes as millions of people followed orders to leave downtown areas, or shelter in place. Fire and ambulance units moved freely, while military columns rolled quickly to their assembly points.

* * *

Commotion migrating up and down the overlapping coastal highways was visible from China's newest aircraft carrier, *Ascendant Prosperity* (*Fāngxīngwèi'ài de fánróng*). High-ranking government officials and popular media figures had been on hand just days earlier to attend the vessel's commissioning ceremony.

The vessel, intended to replace *Strong Prosperity*, was the nation's most modern aircraft carrier. It was at general quarters with little more than a skeleton crew and no aircraft when the second Kodiak formation, designated K-2 on all active navigation plots, passed overhead—beyond the effective range of air defenses that surrounded the city and port.

Chapter Sixteen

Worldwide reaction to the sudden loss of two Chinese aircraft carriers, as witnessed by citizen journalists and untrained observers, was sensational. Audio and video quality of the attacks ranged from excellent to awful as it was streamed on to the internet from expensive digital cameras and smart phones.

News groups, bloggers, and infotainment conglomerates gobbled up every gigabyte of uncensored action as Chinese government agencies and their representatives worked to manage the unfolding crisis. Experts in Beijing watched the Kodiak attack projections converge on Jiuquan, with estimated times of arrival for each pair of ships. Politicians and war planners alike were immediately aware that, for the first time in this conflict, American and Chinese naval forces had parity in aircraft carriers.

"We now have just as many as they do," a well-known logistician explained to members of the Central Committee when consulted by telephone. "With luck, we out-build them, or we sink theirs before they can replace their losses. Either way, this isn't over."

* * *

"Sixty seconds!" Kyle Foss cued.

Beatrice nudged Billy. "I'll start with you."

"Thanks."

Norman looked up from the glowing tablet he was reading. "Amazing," he exclaimed while rolling back in his chair. "Why are they bothering to clamp down?"

"Old habits," she shrugged.

* * *

Administrator Lao saw his military liaison approach through the crimson gloom. "What now?" he fretted.

The uniformed man stopped at a respectful distance to hand him a tablet computer. Andrew took it and saw amateur video images of smoke and fire glitter off the rolling sea within casual view of Shanghai's industrial harbor.

"It's not on any official news feed," the serious man told him, "All indications are that *Ascendant Prosperity* was destroyed."

"These are illegal broadcasts."

The officer nodded gravely. "It's just now 10:45. The elements K-1 and K-2 are now on course for our location. It's not hard to guess—"

Andrew pushed the tablet back in to his officer's chest. "Sweep the complex for threats," he whispered. "Check identities and search all important installations! Hold anyone with questionable documents or out-of-date work orders."

The security chief took the computer in one hand. "Kodiak's first strike gets here in 15 minutes. What are your orders concerning the civilian sectors?"

Lao hesitated. Tossing bars and businesses might reveal any number of hidden activities that he'd be forced to deal with. "Aviation and aerospace only," he decided. "Do what it takes to keep our main mission resources secure and useful. Of course, I will look the other way if you need to teach a lesson to the lawless."

* * *

"Stick to the script!" Raven demanded. Shadows in the darkly furnished office began to feel sinister, making her think the place really did resemble a villain's lair.

"What script?" Kyle complained. "We're jumping from one crisis to the next, thanks to all your last minute directives! I've got the White House press secretary holding on my private line! How'd he get my number? What do I tell him?"

"*Not one word,*" she asserted stonily, "Nobody admits anything until we see what happens to Jiuquan. Follow those directives until I say otherwise, or you're fired!"

"Suppose I hear from the President?"

"Tell him you're busy!" she giggled. "Works for me all the time."

* * *

Sirens wailed across Jiuquan starport. Exterior lighting was turned off to make surface-level facilities harder to see from the air. Thousands of workers and their families went to bunkers and shelters to wait out the expected attack. Police cruisers were dispatched to every major road intersection to ensure the flow of military traffic. Anti-aircraft guns and missile batteries were activated and tied into regional communications networks through encrypted landlines.

Inside hardened underground hangars, aerospace technicians and pilots worked as fast as procedures would permit to prepare both of the surviving space planes for another flight. Two more of the same type were towed out of nearby machine shops. With some fanfare, both ships were taxied into the staging area.

* * *

Andrew Lao watched Beatrice work with grudging admiration as the first pair of aerospace fighters from Kodiak approached Jiuquan Starport. "She acts like nothing is about to happen," he observed dryly.

News from Kodiak was just one of many channels visible on screens around the operations chamber. Andrew studied Brown's body language as she appeared on his podium, projected in miniature with stereo sound.

"Chief of Security Billy Richter is here," she introduced with a smile. "To my right is Kodiak Starport's air defense director, Norman Ahgupuk. Gentlemen, I'd like to ask both of you a few questions about our situation, now that you've had a chance to deal with our most immediate emergencies."

Billy hesitated when a camera zoomed in. "G-good morning, Beatrice. I'm glad to report that most of our fires are…under control. We've had some problems with looting, but it's nothing we can't handle. All things considered, I'd have to say we're quite lucky. What happened here tonight could've been worse."

Lao struck the arm of his chair with an angry fist. His silent rage was interrupted by a phone call from the media department.

"Network representatives are holding air time for you at the top of the hour," a specialist informed him. "In light of what just happened near the coast, they'd like to know if this will be good news. What should we tell them?"

Andrew gathered his thoughts while Beatrice Brown continued her deception. Raven Frost had bluffed him into thinking that Jiuquan Starport would be her only point of interest. That much was now clear to him as Norman Ahgupuk talked so proudly about what it was like to shoot down an enemy aerospace fighter.

"—which is why nobody could see what we were doing!" the enthusiastic aviator recalled with exaggerated hand gestures. "It was a team effort. Everyone from the controllers in our command-and-control bird, to the guys who flew with me. All of 'em beat the odds."

"What happens now?"

The question seemed to confuse Norman. “It’s a new kind of war,” he exhaled. “We’ve always known that space would be the new high ground. Here it is.”

Andrew found himself nodding in silent approval. He turned his attention back to the open phone line that flashed on his console. “Please tell the schedulers that my remarks will be positive. No more than 15 minutes will be necessary.”

The man cleared his throat. “There are unofficial inquiries from unapproved sources. We’re being asked about enemy aerospace fighters.”

“We don’t reply to them,” Lao hissed. “We never respond to those—*ever*!”

“The inbound threat is known. It’s all over the internet.”

Andrew looked up to see the advancing aerospace plots. His heart beat faster. “It’s a new kind of war,” he concurred softly. “Winners make the history. That’s why we’re here, to decide who writes the next chapter.”

“Sir?”

Lao shook off his melancholy with a sudden brusque gesture. “Nothing. I was just considering—doesn’t matter! It’s 11:15. More than enough time to see how this ends. Please inform our networks that I *will* have good news for them at the top of the hour. It’s fitting that we’ll be doing this at midnight.” He smiled. “One way or another, it will mean the start of a new day for somebody.”

* * *

“I really don’t like this!” Beatrice protested by wireless phone during a commercial break. “Why are we treading water?”

The administrator sighed through speakers in the set desk. “All I can say is that we’re nearly there. You see what I see. Things are coming to a boil.”

"What are we waiting for?"

Raven looked at a bank of muted television screens on her office wall. Silent images from Hong Kong and Shanghai changed rapidly. "I…will know it when I see it," she promised. "Big. Big stuff. Anything that mentions Jiuquan."

"Why wasn't I told about this?" Billy asked with an open soda can in one hand.

"Couldn't say before the cat was out of the bag," Frost replied blandly.

"That's quite the kitty," Billy remarked. "We got plowed like a turnip field. I hope you plan on doing more than just returning the favor?"

Beatrice wiped sweat off her forehead. "I'm getting tired of the slow bake," she replied. "Let's worry about who didn't know what after the dust settles. I'm just as much in the dark as you are."

Richter leaned over to put his beverage down. "So. Here we sit, watching the world come unglued—"

"Please!" Raven interrupted. "Billy, you know better. We're all having a bad day. This is what had to be done, turnips and all. It's my call and I made it!"

"Aircraft carriers?"

"Yes," she responded, slowing her voice in an effort to control her temper. "You know the speech. Keep the door open. Nobody flies if we blast each other back to the Stone Age. Somebody has to do the right thing. Might as well be us."

* * *

Major General Xiao Lung stepped off a large wide elevator into a warm, underground command post busy with activity. Consoles and displays around the heavily reinforced compartment filled the room with a surreal glow that he found reassuring, because it meant a constant flow of information was still coming to him.

"How much longer until full mobilization?" he asked the nearest major.

The man replied from a cluttered workstation. "Everything's up now. All formations will be in their assigned orbits within five minutes."

The former pilot went to a large screen flanked by smaller displays, asking Colonel Daniel Daichen to pull up the regional air defense plot. "Here is K-1." He pointed when the screen lit with new data. "There is K-2. We'll do to them what they did to us, only on a larger scale. Kodiak's response was, what? Four interceptors? We'll be meeting them with ten times that, once all four squadrons are up and vectored."

"Our interceptors won't fly as high as theirs did," Daichen elaborated from the other side of the projection. "There is only one good response to our defense. Assuming they came prepared for that option, two separate pairs won't be able to do so much damage to our starport. We think that is deliberate."

"K-1 intercept in seven minutes!"

Lung thought about what he'd seen streaming on the internet and through broadcast media. "This isn't what it looks like," he deduced while his eyes roamed over the air defense map. "Something's going on here that we don't know about."

"Politics?"

"Starports," the general scowled as if he had a bad taste in his mouth, "That one—Kodiak—doesn't read from the nationalist playbook. Explains why they haven't done what we would have in their position."

Daniel pointed to a nearby small hologram. "Several of us agree with you. The fact that they attacked our carriers without inflicting further damage on the battle groups does suggest a desire to change the balance of power, with no guidance from Washington."

"Mercenary!" Xiao spat.

Daichen hesitated. "Doesn't matter, if it works."

"What happens to Jiuquan?"

"W-we think it'll be mild."

The implications made Xiao pause to survey the moods of those around him. Every officer and specialist was conveniently looking somewhere else, doing something else that appeared to keep them busy.

"Were you elected or did you volunteer?"

"I thought you should hear this from me," he responded diplomatically.

"I see," the general acknowledged without emotion. He turned away for several seconds to think without revealing any facial expressions to anyone who might be watching. "We're not going to shoot them down?"

Daniel chose his words carefully. "The unorthodox manner of this operation suggests that we won't. It's quite likely that they are going to do something else we haven't planned for."

Xiao faced his subordinate. "I appreciate your insight and your initiative. Activate the black line to Beijing. I want to speak with my superiors, unofficially. If what you have to say is convincing, I may ask you to repeat it."

"Unofficially?"

"Completely off the record."

Chapter Seventeen

Eyewitness reaction to events in Hong Kong and Shanghai made for controversial reportage around the world. Media outlets of every stripe put their own spins on what was happening in China, creating a climate of confusion. Amateur video added to the sensationalism of many broadcasts. Tabloid journalism surged in popularity as unlikely estimates were thrown around concerning Chinese naval casualties, which were exaggerated to the point of absurdity by some news organizations.

Bloggers and independent commentators were more flexible and insightful than their mainstream counterparts. As surprised as many viewers were by the sudden destruction of two state-of-the-art aircraft carriers, they weren't fully aware of what those losses meant.

"It's not the speed," an Indonesian host related to his television audience, "it's how this was done. That's what we should be paying attention to. Can we run those images again?"

With no firsthand sightings of the aerospace attack, or any solid evidence on video, survivors and observers alike were left to ponder the source. Military experts openly agreed that both capital ships must've been destroyed by supersonic space planes dropping kinetic strike weapons. Some conspiracy theorists went so far as to suggest that this unexpected event was the result of flying saucers armed with disintegration rays.

"The only question is," a popular international talk show host pondered dramatically. "Who's controlling them? Are they friend or foe?"

* * *

Raven watched a red light flash on the administrator's hotline for three full pulses before she answered the encrypted call from Joint Base Wainwright-Eielson.

"General Sachdeva," she began solicitously. "How are things?"

"I wish they could be better," Manika replied regretfully. "You've put on quite the show. I'm wondering if you still have room for dessert."

"Always."

Sachedva paused. "I think there is good news," she said obliquely. "I have analysis coming through channels now, saying there is a high probability of military aerospace activity. That means they won't ask."

"Why so unsure?" Frost worried.

Manika settled in her chair. "Corporation-on-corporation violence is one thing. They'd understand that. Even if one of them is a state-sponsored actor. You have…"

"Gone off the script?" Raven offered.

"Yes," the general accepted. "I don't suppose you can let me in on how this ends?"

The administrator looked at the memorabilia hanging on the walls around her dimly lit office. "You know how it is," she side-stepped with false modesty. "Better villains don't brag about the nuts and bolts of their plans so close to the end. Save that for later."

"Is that how you see yourself?"

"Washington can't approve of what we do," the embattled executive responded without remorse. "Even if we're successful, that's not how things are done. Too many cooks do more than spoil the soup. They make the recipe unpopular. So, here we are, doing what we can with what we've got. Let the historians sort it out."

* * *

Turning and climbing away from their primary targets, the Kodiak aerospace formations raced over northeastern China toward Mongolian airspace and the Gobi Desert. Airborne lidars and sporadic ground-based radar contacts left few doubts about the number of ships, or their course and speed.

Military and political analysts in Beijing agreed that the next target appeared to be Jiuquan Starport. Consensus fractured when working groups were tasked with projecting potential damage from the anticipated attack. "We have to assume they get through," a senior official warned when his questions went unanswered, "They're attacking with reduced payloads. How much harm can they really do?"

Intelligence experts were just as divided in their opinions. Every minute of broadcast coverage from Kodiak Starport was still being examined for clues that would verify what local sources communicated to their handlers in the form of audio, video, and text messages. Results of these comparisons were inconsistent, suggesting that Beatrice Brown's version of events was not entirely accurate.

"Don't rely on any of it," a media consultant reminded her high-ranking audience when arguments became heated. "We show them what we want them to see. They do the same, with a little more sex and violence. Words and pictures influence millions. They always have. If you will please turn to page six of my report, you will see that I prepared a few options. Several responses are possible…"

* * *

American planners and politicians were just as uncertain about events unfolding in the sky over China.

Broadcast media was so contradictory that some analysts stopped watching and reading. Others made a sincere effort to separate fact from fiction by comparing what they *did* know with what they *didn't* know. Acting on the assumption that journalistic error and commercial misrepresentation were no different than misinformation, they worked to screen it out at every level of the assessment process.

Beijing's ongoing crisis encouraged a wait-and-see attitude. The widely sensationalized loss of two capital warships was easy to verify. Implications were obvious and immediate. In just a few heart-stopping seconds, the opponent's numerical advantage in aircraft carriers was gone. "It's not a total shift in our favor," Navy analysts concurred in coded communications. "It won't win the war for us, but it does level the playing field."

* * *

Andrew Lao put on a light jacket emblazoned with golden company logos. "Let's go for a walk," he told his assigned guard.

Together, they rode up to ground level in an armored elevator. His protector was dressed in the uniform of an officer and carried a government-issue sidearm. Both men strode through a deserted lobby, up two flights of stairs, into a silent conference room. It was a journey they'd made before.

"Five minutes," the starport executive requested, swiping his ID card through an electronic reader to open an armored door at the far end of the long, quiet room.

"I'm not so sure this is a good idea," the lieutenant said worriedly.

"Relax" Andrew objected wryly. "I'm not going to jump!"

"Sir, please—"

"Five minutes," Lao repeated while stepping through the door in to darkness. It shut behind him with an audible click. From a second-story concrete balcony, he saw empty streets and darkened buildings in all directions, each blacked out against the threat of air attack.

Andrew shivered while surveying the industrial landscape. Taking a compact phone from his coat pocket, he called his wife. The wireless device chirped through an encrypted dialing sequence, ringing three times before a sleepy feminine voice answered.

They spoke tenderly for several minutes. "Don't worry about what you see on television," he admonished kindly. "Everything will be sorted out by morning."

"Are you going to be on the news?"

"You would know if I was," he responded pleasantly while reading the digital clock on his phone. "Family, friends, and the neighbors would be calling."

* * *

Andrew went back inside two minutes later. He and his guard went to the waiting elevator that would take them back down to the operations amphitheater.

"My wife would like to know if you and your family can visit for the holiday."

"Thank you," the officer accepted graciously as they got off the elevator deep underground. "They will enjoy that, very much!"

"How long to rearm the aerospace group?" Lao asked an aide who suddenly appeared in the hallway.

The observant man held up a tablet for easy reading. "One hour and fifteen minutes," he motioned. "They are faster than usual."

"Motivated," Andrew acknowledged, taking off his jacket.

In the operations chamber, he stopped by his office to leave his coat on a chair. Approaching the local air defense projection with a practiced posture intended to broadcast confidence, he looked around for more information. Aviation estimates on a dozen consoles provided planners and controllers with facts and figures about the expanding air defense envelope beyond the geographic boundaries of Jiuquan Prefecture.

Knowing that his behavior mattered in a stressful situation, he made a show of studying the slowly rotating hologram in the center of a massive table. Technicians and specialists came closer when he spoke. All four special duty squadrons were marked. Air traffic control frequencies chattered in the background as controllers directed each formation to increasingly higher altitudes that would allow them to protect the southern approaches to Gensu Province.

"K-1 arrives in four minutes," the administrator observed from scrolling notations next to each inbound threat marker. "K-2 is just two minutes behind. See how their approach vectors are converging? K-1 has reduced speed. K-2 has accelerated. They intend to merge just before entering our airspace."

"Arrogant marauders!" somebody quipped.

"Dead men," Andrew pronounced grimly. "As you can see, we have four special duty squadrons orbiting at altitudes ranging from 60,000 to 90,000 feet. That corkscrew pattern lets them cover a lot of sky. They're all equipped with missiles that reach into space."

"Intruder formations have merged!"

"Doesn't matter," Lao declared in an effort to banish his own dread. "They've given up any stealth advantage they had. Ground-based tracking has had an eye on them for quite some time. Our high altitude observers can see them, too."

His military liaison shuffled in close. “They want to be seen,” he theorized. “Seven hundred miles and closing. They’ll be over the horizon, in our airspace—”

“It does not matter,” Andrew interjected succinctly. “They’ll be intercepted so far away from here that we will never see or hear any of it.”

* * *

The Kodiak aerospace fighters spread out in a staggered line as they cruised near the edge of space. Pilot banter through short range encrypted radio was animated.

“Hold course and speed for 50 seconds,” North Wind ordered as the flight leader commented, “Damn, that was a kick in the pants!”

“Pants?” East Wind laughed while reading his instruments, “I was aimin’ for that aircraft carrier snuggled up to Hong Kong. Nothin’ in my target set about trousers, pants, or shorts. Who messed up?”

“No time for tourism,” West Wind lamented. “South, check your interval. Not so close, man. My wife is the jealous kind. We should be visible to anything that’s up there taking pictures. Too bad we can’t wave or give ‘em the bird.”

“Falling back 20,” South Wind signaled from the rear of the formation.

North Wind remained all business. “Descent in 30 seconds. Let your detectors watch for incoming. It’ll be ASMs or high fliers with a death wish, trying to get lucky with guns. Any questions?”

* * *

The administrator stared at the local air defense plot in silent awe.

"Amazing," Andrew conceded as tiny numbers on the display changed faster than a human eye could read.

"Threat is descending!" a technician repeated.

"Is that a powered dive?" he asked from his podium.

The military liaison looked to both of his aviation analysts for some input. They merely shrugged. "They are supersonic, so it really doesn't matter," he concluded. "Present range is 530 miles, which gives them line of sight on our facility from their present altitude—and they're coming in below our fighters!"

Lao reached for a red telephone handset. "What is the status of our lockdown?"

"All departments report ready!" a defense coordinator announced. "Civilian workers have reported to shelters. Military checkpoints are manned and ready!"

The starport boss raised his handset. "Air defense," a stern voice answered. "All systems online and ready for action! What are your orders?"

"Active search; fire on anything that's not supposed to be here!"

* * *

Military observation systems impartially recorded the Kodiak aerospace fighters' evasion of the armada that circled Jiuquan Starport. Cameras and sensors onboard drones and aircraft throughout the region recorded the formation's extraordinary drop in altitude prior to the release of the crafts' payloads. Satellites in high orbit followed the progress of all four ships through a high-gravity turn that sent them in a northeasterly direction, away from the squadrons assigned to stop them.

Civilian drones owned by a dozen different media conglomerates operating at lower altitudes caught fleeting thermal traces and brief video images of the fast moving space planes as they vanished over the moonlit Mongolian horizon, in to predawn Siberian airspace.

Ground-based radars and lidar-equipped installations had no difficulty tracking the inbound kinetic strikes that approached Jiuquan starport in plunging arcs. Each 6,000-pound rocket-assisted weapon was optically guided by a series of onboard computers that controlled tail fins to steer the falling rods into their predesignated targets based on what they saw while passing over roads, buildings, and other landmarks.

Independent commentary appeared on the internet when Jiuquan Starport's air defense artillery lit up the night. Millions of tracer bullets, fired from hundreds of multi-barrel emplacements and tracked vehicles, filled the sky. Streams of red, yellow, and green reached for different altitudes, based on the limitations of each gun's caliber. Illegal video verified this happening with some sensationalism and uncensored language as bold men and women risked losing their jobs to view the fireworks through the high-resolution cameras in their smart phones.

* * *

"Is that what we've been waiting for?" Norman guessed as three different small screens flashed with breaking news.

"Wow," Billy exclaimed when crawls read 'Jiuquan Starport,' along with various claims of assault, massacre, and attack.

"That *is* us, isn't it?" Beatrice asked blandly.

Raven's voice broadcast through the set desk. "Yes!" she cheered. "That's us! Definitely us! That, or some of those flying saucers I was just reading about."

The journalist rolled back in her chair. "That was a lot of hype just to tell me we're killin' 'em."

Norman snorted with a mixture of fatigue and discontent. "Hype is what we've been doing while those carriers went to the bottom. So, let me guess. Now it's time for a few minutes of live television?"

* * *

Military police were sent to every corner of Jiuquan Starport to combat the growing media menace. Leaping out of cars and trucks, they searched the entire complex with direction from political activity coordinators, in an effort to stop unauthorized transmissions from reaching clandestine "piggy back" internet providers, who shared what they found with the world. Some of these blustery bureaucrats and bellicose law enforcers were taunted by the people they arrested just before cameras were smashed, adding to the drama that excited prurient interests around the world.

* * *

The administrator's podium shook with vibrations from distant impacts. Crimson lighting flickered as emergency condition indicators flashed warnings in a remote corner of the starport.

"How close?"

His military liaison used a remote control wand to prioritize damage assessments on an overhead display. "They hit our aerospace maintenance terminal and both of the adjoining underground launch corridors. Fire crews are responding."

Andrew looked up at the vaulted ceiling to read the changing details. "Am I reading that correctly? Are the auxiliary runways also caved in?"

"Both of them," the officer conceded squeamishly.

Lao began to sweat when he realized that all of his aerospace assets were grounded. He was about to give an order when a government phone line buzzed. He answered quickly. "General Lung, the Kodiak strike force is—"

"Shut up and listen," Xiao demanded.

"Sir."

The general harrumphed. "Administrator, we have just seen a little bit of the old and some of what's new. Strategy and innovation. Guts and gadgets."

"Yes."

"Listen very carefully," Xiao emphasized. "*I* don't hold you responsible for what just happened. Others may not be so generous. Some effort on your part may be required."

"I understand."

"Good," he replied more cordially. "Put a lid on this and you could still be a hero, even if it means making a gesture."

Andrew hung up without responding to the hint. Raven Frost's insult made him angry when he remembered it. "We'll see who resigns," he mumbled to himself while standing up. "Tell the air defense to cease fire! Have the manned patrols reinforced with dogs. Sweep every sector! Authorize armed robots for any squad that wants them! Department heads, give me an update in five minutes. We have a press conference to manage."

Chapter Eighteen

Global opinion relating to events unfolding in northeastern China evolved as new details emerged. Activists of all sorts throughout the desert region called on seldom-trusted associates to make the most of the moment. Infotainment conglomerates around the world struggled to cope with a sudden flood of freelance video from these unexpected sources. Executives in charge of content distribution met behind closed doors to review what many considered to be the most controversial offerings before approving them for broadcast.

Chinese corporate media was just as circumspect. Government officials were reluctantly impressed by the quality and quantity of illegal material they seized.

"Years of campaigning against irresponsible opinionating have apparently failed," a Beijing commentator scolded her late night radio audience. "This is not the way civilized people should behave!"

Tabloid-style programming focused on the obvious fact that three starports had been attacked in less than 12 hours. Lurid narration introduced action-oriented images from all three locations as lead-ins to panel discussions. Topics ranged from sinister to silly as hosts probed for inspirational answers.

"What does this mean for the future safety of the Russian facility at Baikonur?" many panelists pondered at nearly the same time.

"The situation at Jiuquan is unclear. If Alaska and Japan are any indication, we—humanity—are on the verge of losing spaceflight as we know it."

* * *

"They are…gone," General Lung observed from his underground bunker. "That maneuver is a message. Very smart. They've made their point and now are going home."

"Why so conspicuous about it?" his aide murmured without taking his eyes off a digital air defense map.

The old aviator clucked his disapproval. "You're the one who warned me about what was happening. Why don't you see this for what it is?"

Daniel turned his back on the combat projection. He faced his superior with a more respectful demeanor. "They were creative," he accepted with some regret. "We can be ready for them if they come back."

"Not if," Xiao amended tersely. "It's only a matter of time. Back to Alaska. Refuel and rearm, just like we intended to."

"Engineers?"

Lung scoffed. "Those runways were hidden for a reason. It'll take three days for any good construction battalion to clear that much debris. Then there's the matter of—never mind! It's pointless. Somebody has to make a deal."

"What—"

The senior officer raised his hand. "You've had your say. If this problem escalates, we won't have a starport to defend. Kodiak will see to that. Our government will have to reach an accommodation with them. I can only hope nothing has been done behind the scenes to compromise our diplomats."

The colonel took a step closer. "We can't just—"

"We must!" Xiao swore. "If it doesn't end here and now, while we still have something to bargain with, we lose the war! Give me a few minutes to think. I need to speak with Administrator Lao before he does anything unfortunate."

* * *

Tempers in the television studio on Kodiak Island became heated as telephones, control panels, and automated video editors demanded more attention from their human operators. Nobody behind the production line needed to be told that what they saw happening halfway around the world was a direct result of the earlier tragedies in downtown Anchorage. Lurid gossip magnified the impact of what they saw on international channels to foment tension throughout the building.

A short commercial break faded. Beatrice Brown looked at the nearest camera without making any attempt to hide her weariness. "Welcome back to our live coverage. Early reports of damage to Chinese aircraft carriers near Hong Kong and Shanghai are being validated by independent sources. Both of these events are being denied by mainland government agencies, in spite of mounting evidence to the contrary."

Pictures from well-known networks and several underground newsgroups around the world filled visual fields as she spoke. "I'm now able to confirm through my own sources that these were high altitude precision attacks, carried out by space planes launched from our own Kodiak Starport. With me now to explain in greater detail are security chief Billy Richter and air defense coordinator Norman Ahgupuk."

Andrew Lao was conferring with a group of engineers when he was interrupted by his secretary.

"Administrator Frost is calling."

He handed a tablet computer to the nearest man. "Finish this and get back to me," he ordered while stepping away from the group.

"Would you like to take this call in your office?" his assistant asked as she followed.

"No," he replied grudgingly while walking up the steps of his podium to sit in the high backed chair. "I'll take this here." He turned, looking for his facility manager. "Normal area lighting, please! Reduce our alert level and update the schedule. Night shift reports for duty in a few minutes. I don't want anything to interfere with the changeover!"

Nearby, a portly man wearing a green vest with electronic devices in each hand signaled his understanding with a wave. Overhead, lighting faded from red to soft white as the administrator reached for a blue telephone handset and typed in his authorization code. "Administrator Frost, it has been a long night."

"For both of us."

Andrew glanced at his desk displays and the reports coming in from inspectors around Jiuquan Starport. Local time on a digital clock read 11:55 p.m. "This isn't what I expected. Nothing like what I thought it would be."

"I know."

"Did you have any idea it would work out like this?" he inquired, just to avoid anything more unpleasant.

Alone in her office, Raven got out of her chair and began to pace while speaking through her wireless earpiece. "My planes have just come back into our airspace. They'll be landing soon. I can have them back in your sky before anyone has time to—"

"Yes," he interrupted, "I'm sure your government will be pleased."

"It's not their decision," she asserted. "It'll be ours, if we do it."

Lao felt a knot grow in his stomach. "Does that mean what I think it does?"

"It does," she replied.

"What did you have in mind?"

Raven came to a stop near several portraits of past administrators. They hung on a wall near the door in silver frames. Not so obvious to visitors. Always visible to anyone who sat in the executive's chair. What did Lao actually know about the actions taken by his government?

"Shut down for the next two years," she tendered emotionlessly. "I mean it. Pull the plug on everything. Don't even fly a kite for the next 24 months! Of course, you will resign, as publicly as possible."

Andrew looked from one side of the amphitheater to the other, at the dozens of men and women who would be affected by this evening's outcome. Frost's tone of voice suggested to him that she was acting on information he didn't have. "This is not my decision to make," he replied slowly.

"You can prevent any more damage to your starport."

Her words made him reticent because they reflected the sentiment expressed by General Lung in a phone call he'd suffered through just a few minutes earlier. His political instincts warned that this convergence of industrial considerations was no ordinary coincidence. He'd never been a factory manager, though he did understand the value of high-tech facilities and what it could mean to lose them permanently.

"I'm not in a position to negotiate," he stalled.

"You've taken more than I'm asking for," she said sharply. "You're not the decision-maker, Mr. Lao, but you are the messenger! Those are my terms. Give us an answer soon. All my ships will be armed, fueled, and on their way before your superiors can decide to bother us with ICBMs."

"I hardly think—"

"That much is obvious!" she shouted, stomping out her frustration with one foot. "Just remember, we have no satellite communications. I won't be able to recall our strike beyond a certain point."

* * *

Formal news anchors and casual commentators alike were surprised by Kodiak Starport's admission when Brown's remarks reached them.

"It amounts to a declaration of war," some of them decided on the air without any attempt to break for editorial considerations.

Others did pause to confer with savvy ratings managers and objective board members before proceeding.

"Have we just seen corporatism run amok?" they probed cautiously, "or is this a new phase in the conflict with blessings from Washington?"

These questions, and many more like them, did more than spark debates. They were leveraged by networks and advertisers to encourage audiences by e-mail and texting services to participate in opinion polls. Arguments made on-air by personalities with large followings caused factions to form in social media communities. Passionate participants in every time zone had it out with each other through social media and various legal challenges. Details, large and small, were publicized as allegations were made or found to be plausible during lengthy investigations.

Program ratings soared for syndicated shows that could keep pace with the rapidly developing situation. Alaskan infotainers were given a two-minute head start by insiders at the Kodiak Starport.

"Seems only fair to let it come from a local source," one of them told an Anchorage radio personality. "How many times have you been left out in the cold? Don't quote me, but—"

Language was quickly copied and adopted when American and Chinese press releases circulated. Government representatives and former military personnel from other nations weren't eager to presage the final outcomes of what was so obviously a vigorous, ongoing operation.

Civilian analysts, who were answerable to no one, had no such reservations about what they saw. Many of them had already been on a tear that evening about what was happening.

"Are they right?" a Canadian presenter asked worriedly, straying off script. "Tokyo starport is no more. Kodiak is in ruins. Now we hear about Jiuquan being under attack. Are we losing our grip on the moon and the stars?"

* * *

"Not if I can help it," Raven vowed under her breath while watching the same broadcast from atop her dais in the underground operations center.

Canadian, British, and Indonesian broadcasts played on small screens in her field of view. "Mr. Allison!" she demanded while typing orders to department heads. "Where is Nanook?"

The launch coordinator walked to the base of her platform with a tablet in each hand. "They're in our airspace now," he indicated by waving one of the small computers. "It's 5:58. Shift change is in two minutes. D'you really want to do this?"

Frost finished what she was doing before bounding down to the floor in six quick strides. "Next shift comes on as normal," she told him. "Dismiss these fine people any way you like so we can keep the ball rolling."

Andre smirked impishly under the shine of full spectrum lights. He gave his tablets to a passing engineer, then reached for the whistle that hung around his neck. Shuffling away from Raven, he looked for a digital clock. Faces turned in his directed when he blew three sharp tweets. "Graveyard!" he announced proudly. "Your work day is over in 60 seconds! Section leaders, be nice to the morning crew! They missed all the fun!"

Chapter Nineteen

The Kodiak aerospace formation descended gradually through Russian airspace that was still devoid of military radar coverage. Their flightpaths brought all four space planes downward through zones known to be filled with fewer falling particles from low orbit. In spite of this caution, all of the ships were hit by some wreckage that degraded their performance.

Passing over Little Diomede Island, they flew over southwestern Alaska, through regions affected by the Small Rock mining disaster, towards Kodiak Island. Command-and-control aircraft in the southern half of the state reported sightings as they occurred.

Fuel considerations, more than any desire to show off, prompted the flight to reduce speed and altitude. Civilian photographers on the Kenai Peninsula amazed friends, family, and employers by capturing high-resolution images from handheld cameras on the ground and at sea as the aerospace fighters passed overhead.

* * *

When they were in telecommunications range of Gatekeeper, all four planes transmitted their collected sensor data and attack camera video archives to the waiting 747. Enthusiastic technicians forwarded the encrypted information to a ground station inside the starport's smoke-filled perimeter, where it was decoded and sent to various departments for immediate evaluation. Media experts reviewed what they were given as it streamed in.

The formation spread out as the ships approached the Shelikof Strait and the starport's recently plowed network of paved and lighted runways. Crossing over the water between mainland Alaska and Kodiak Island, the fighters deployed speed brakes and parachutes to decelerate, sending a shockwave in all directions that rattled windows and shook furniture.

* * *

Billy Richter let an armored door close before entering the massive operations area with a uniformed aide nearby. His face could be seen on a dozen screens and projections near the administrator's dais as he approached the raised platform.

"It's just now 6:15," his adjutant warned, tapping his own wristwatch. "We're cutting it close."

"Stay here," Richter insisted softly. "I only need five minutes."

"Everything we do here is defensive in nature," his replayed image emphasized as Norman sat quietly in the background. "Our mission is peaceful spaceflight. Nothing more. Preserving that capability means a lot to everyone who works here."

"Do you still believe that?" Raven asked him from her high-backed chair.

He looked up at her from the bottom step. "Nobody had to write those words for me. I didn't like having to read them off a screen. How much damage have we really done to Jiuquan?"

"Negligible," she shrugged.

"Really?"

Raven came down to floor and pointed to a holographic projection of Jiuquan Starport. "Remember what you said about breaking rules?" she reminded him while laying a hand on the slowly turning diagram. "It was my turn and I did it."

Billy came closer to examine the layout. "They can't fly their spaceplanes?"

"Not for at least a week," she appraised.

He bent over to read scrolling data as it appeared on the Chinese model. "We can't make rocket fuel for the next year and half," he groaned. "Never mind the rest of it, which includes the main firehouse and auxiliary engine stations. Both of them. Half of Boom Town is gone, too. How's that a fair trade?"

"I thought our fires were under control?"

Richter stood up. "Nothing about this evening has been under control since it started," he critiqued mildly. "We're getting help from every fire department between here and Fairbanks that can airlift a water bottle or mail a spittoon. So. What's next? Do we burn 'em to the ground, now that they can't fly?"

"That *is* what they expect," Raven conjectured without looking at Billy. "It's what we can do, if it comes down to that."

"You're hoping they do something else?"

"I am," she confided. "That's been the plan all along, even before Jim was promoted. These aerospace things have been in development for a long time. A lot people have known what they could do—would do, if used to their full potential. It's monstrous. He…we…both of us thought we'd be the ones to keep this option under lock and key. I never believed for a minute that I'd have to use them."

Billy walked around the hologram to inspect every aspect of Jiuquan Starport, as it was thought to be according to western intelligence sources. "If they really can't launch or land aerospace, we can go back there and wreck 'em. Air bases here, here, and here," he said, gesturing as he came to a stop next to her. "They'll be smarter next time. A bit more spread out. Even if we have more ships to reinforce the next attack, some of them will be shot down. Bet money on that!"

"If it comes to that..."

Richter was about to speak when an excited man erupted into view.

"You'll want to see this," he told Raven, handing her a tablet.

She showed Billy the computer. The busy technician excused himself.

Raven touched the screen to activate a live news feed. Andrew Lao's face appeared, surrounded by Jiuquan Starport logos and factoids.

"Next question please," he continued in English from behind a lectern. "I apologize for this late start. Our damage control measures have kept me busy. Some consultation with my government was necessary."

* * *

Cameras turned to a round-faced Korean man wearing glasses holding an old fashioned pen and a pad of stenographic paper. "Your opening statement says you are stepping down from your post. Could you be more specific about the reasons?"

Lao's image came back in to frame. Voices murmured. "Our facility will be undergoing extensive refits over the next two years to improve defenses and increase space launch capability," he stated blandly. "My expertise will be necessary to ensure that those upgrades are carried out on time and on budget. I'm sorry if my statement didn't make that clear to you."

"Are you capitulating?" the reporter asked directly.

"No," Andrew responded forcefully. "In just a moment, you'll hear from an official representative of my government. He will tell you that there have been no official demands for the surrender of this facility, nor is there any future threat against this starport. What's done here today is...well, it's done."

"Why?" the same fellow asked.

The audience murmured at what seemed rudeness.

General Xiao Lung, in dress uniform and with a chest full of medals, stepped up to lay a hand on the administrator's shoulder. "Let me answer. Sir, I want to assure all of you that what happened here was anticipated, expected, and planned for. Our response to it may seem reserved, or even a little too kind for western minds to consider, but it is our decision. My country will defend our interests. Our people won't close the door on a part of human history that may never come again."

* * *

Billy looked at Raven skeptically. "All that from a few holes in the ground?"

"Yep," she replied, smiling as she turned off the tablet.

"Is that what you were hoping for?" he inquired as a cheer went up around the room.

"Yes," she shouted to be heard over the din.

"What next?"

Raven looked at the computer in her hands, then at Richter. "Put out a few more fires. Everybody and his brother has seen Nanook, so there's no point in hiding it. We'll make a big deal out of them after they land."

Richter rubbed his chin. "Norman talked me through some of this. Refuel and rearm. Add a few more planes to the roster, then go back for more."

"If we must," she resisted.

"You're getting what you wanted. It's not world peace, but it does keep that precious door open. What more do you want?"

Raven turned the gleaming watch on her wrist when it chafed. "I don't want any man, woman, or child to look up at the night sky in fear. That's what I want, Billy. Now, if you don't mind, I have to call

Washington. The President owes us a favor and I'm going to cash in."

* * *

Audio, video, and text messages of all sorts from a variety of credible sources had been scrutinized by independent media outlets by the time Kodiak's aerospace fighters landed. Chinese government representatives were forced to admit that Jiuquan Starport hadn't suffered as much damage as previously claimed. In the hour that followed, this retraction was more than enough to satisfy some conspiracy theorists.

Controversy collided with tragedy as deaths and injuries were investigated and made public by thousands of corporate and citizen journalists in search of their own truths. Tempests erupted locally, nationally, and internationally, at every level of social discourse, as people in every nation decided how these incidents mattered, if they were affected at all. Behind the scenes, American and Chinese diplomats met face-to-face in Switzerland for an urgent discussion of their options.

"We are recommending a cease fire to negotiate an end to overall hostilities," the senior U.S. delegate indicated while sitting across from his counterpart in a secured luxury suite. "No change of borders at this time. All ships at sea will return to their respective ports. Land formations will disengage from fighting and stop where they are. Air forces will restrict their movement to sovereign airspace, with the exception of unarmed transportation. All other arrangements are to be made at a later date."

The leading Chinese diplomat listened, then conferred by telephone with his colleagues. "This offer has a short time limit?"

"It does."

There was no need for anyone to explain what would happen if such an unspecified deadline expired. Both men were aware of Raven Frost's private ultimatum and what it would mean for the futures of their nations.

"They wouldn't succeed a second time," the Chinese ambassador objected, speaking into the telephone handset. "Yes. I understand. I'll be here." He gave the handset to a waiting aide and looked at his adversary. "I can see that this does not sit well with you. May I ask why?"

The American shifted in his chair. "C'mon. You know better than that. This decision has already been made. We're just messengers. Our opinions don't count for much at this point in the process. All we've got to do now is make this happen, one way or the other. Smoothly. Haven't seen you since Iran. What's new?"

Changing the subject, they talked about more pleasant things for half an hour. Memories of exotic places and hijinks during early diplomatic postings were interrupted by the return of a ringing telephone.

"Yes?" the senior Chinese diplomat answered while his assistant waited. "I understand completely. Yes. I'll get back to you in a few minutes." He gave his handset back to the silent man, who left the room.

"My government agrees. Please ask your State Department to begin protocols. If you would put in a good word for me, I may be of service."

* * *

"Come here," an exhausted Kyle Foss urged an equally worn out Beatrice Brown. "I have something to show you.'

She looked up from her messy desk. "Record it and I'll watch later."

"Trust me," he implored while swaying in the open door. "You want to see this while it's happening."

Beatrice took off her jacket and threw it aside while wobbling to her feet. "I keep expecting that lousy phone to ring," she complained as they walked down the empty corridor.

"Not going to happen," he joked. "I abused my prerogatives and did something terrible to the switchboard. Maintenance will have to fix it after somebody has the good sense to make a report. Too bad I sent the clerical staff home as a holiday gesture."

"Good supervisors do that sort of thing," she rejoined facetiously while following him into his hot, noisy control room.

Foss pulled his necktie off while pointing limply at a bank of color monitors. "Tomorrow's rock stars," he declared over the heads of four busy technicians, "complete with photos, backstory, and cameos by local personalities. All you have to do is cherry pick what you want after a few hours of sleep and run with it."

"That is priceless," Beatrice choked when she saw dozens of reporters and camera operators from around the world mobbing Norman Ahgupuk and his pilots around a trio of parked F-15s. "It's fantastic! Who put that together?"

Kyle snorted. "The boss has been one step ahead of us all night," he said admiringly through his weariness. "The borough mayor is out there, somewhere. A source I trust informs me that Governor Wheeler is on his way, coming down from Fairbanks. Should be here in about four hours. That ought to be just enough time for you to catch a nap."

"Where are the big deal space planes?"

"I wouldn't know," he responded stiffly, "though we did see them land through about 50 different cameras. And all of it was cleared for you to use, except the part where they go single-file into what looks like—"

"Yeah, yeah, yeah," Beatrice waved as if clearing smoke. "I'll be in my office having that nap. Wake me in two hours!"

CHAPTER TWENTY

Governor Sheldon Wheeler spent most of the day before Christmas seeing the damage at the Kodiak Starport for himself, in between meetings with Raven Frost and members of her senior staff. Photographers and camera trucks weren't far away when he walked through what was left of the civilian sector known as 'Boom Town,' or later, driving through the vast expanse of what had been the launch complex's multipurpose chemical refining plant.

Dressed for the cold, wearing a parka with state logos, he met with an exclusive contingent of Alaskan media representatives in a closed hangar under tight security, next to one of the starport's modified F-15s. "I've been on the phone with the State Department two times in the last ten hours," Sheldon told them while sitting on the fender of a snowplow. "Administrator Frost assures me that she'll give us her full cooperation. I need to know what happened here so that every resource can be used to make things right."

"What about Anchorage?" somebody asked.

"The mayor is a personal friend of mine," Wheeler assured amiably. "I've been in contact with them, too. My staff has been awake all night, like most of you. Tomorrow is Christmas. Please, give us a few days to work on this! Don't be so quick to judge, based on what you think about all this, right now. Find your facts and then dig for a few more."

* * *

Journalists and politicians had more to think about on Christmas Day, when a joint American and Chinese delegation met in New York City, at the United Nations building, to announce the start of cease fire negotiations. Reading from prepared statements, representatives from the two countries expressed yuletide sentiments and wishes for a "reasoned and considerate end to the conflict."

Formal terms for a suspension of hostilities were agreed to and signed into effect on New Year's Eve. "This does not end the war," Japan's Prime Minister acknowledged during the signing ceremony in Beijing. "Even so, it is a start. For the sake of what we have lost, and what could still be no more, we must reach for peace. A parched and hungry world demands it."

Public opinion throughout the Asia-Pacific Rim reflected similar positive sentiments when commercial media reported on the withdrawal of American and Chinese warships from contested zones. Drones and manned aircraft circled ships and surfaced submarines when they were within range, sending video back to land-based commentators who had a lot to say about what looked like an end to the world's most bitter war.

Holiday sentiment faded with the start of a new year. The realities of wrangling over the monetary value of injuries, deaths, and cultural losses proved to be too much for some negotiators. These political and diplomatic casualties made repatriation of seized lands that much harder when new faces met for the first time, attempting to regain the trust that had been lost.

Comedians around the world began referring to recent events as "that war without a surrender," even though many of their national leaders were hailing it as something more positive.

"We have seen two instances of Hell on this continent," the U.K.'s Prime Minister observed pithily. "Let's give them credit for putting this fire out before it spread. One blitz is enough for my history book, thank you."

Diplomats and leaders representing the allies of both combatants were just as relieved to be part of a de-escalation, rather than partners in a new phase of violence. Peace talks dragged on into March before both sides had a framework they could live with. Unlike past wars, this compact would take decades to implement because so many treaties had been broken beyond anyone's understanding.

Apologies, reparations, and restitutions, if any were possible, would be harder to achieve because modern communications were so fast and far-reaching. Old beliefs clashed with new ideas so frequently in the arena of global social media that outrage sparked before, during, and after the war would continue to drown out voices of compromise for years to come.

Civic-minded activists, who had been questioning the role of corporate media throughout the conflict, focused some of their critical attention on Beatrice Brown when she received awards for her journalism.

"Why is she being rewarded for skillful omission?" a well-known essayist complained. "The whiz-bang we saw and heard from her while all that technology was in motion came from just one source, meant to dazzle. Why isn't anyone looking more closely at what she didn't say when she could have?"

* * *

Alaskan meteorologists announced the early arrival of spring when westerly winds from Japan and the South Pacific combined to create a broad warm front that swept over the central region of the state in late March, lingering through mid-April to accelerate thawing. There wasn't any trace of snow on Kodiak Island when lawyers and insurance adjusters from a dozen financially distressed firms finished their appraisals of damage at the space launch complex.

"Payouts are going to be massive," an accountant told Raven Frost as he got off an elevator. Dressed in a black pantsuit and full-length overcoat, she put on a pair of sunglasses in the underground parking garage before getting into a large, blue SUV with starport logos. "Don't let all those numbers make you crazy," she told the conservatively dressed man while reaching for a seatbelt. "We're going to spend all of that to put this place back together. Get back to me when you've got a more comprehensive summary. Make sure it includes the new space station."

An armed guard stepped in close to shut her door. Members of her staff, bodyguard detail, and entourage scattered to find their own assigned rides before the 30-vehicle motorcade got underway. Rolling out of the darkness on to a midday street bathed in sunlight from a clear blue sky, the procession snaked its way out of the starport's ordered interior, through cleared corridors of cavernous excavation and skeletal, multistory construction, onto a freshly paved coastal road swarming with bystanders.

Planned weeks earlier, the big budget televised event was presented to the world by Kyle Foss, who chatted with a worldwide audience through social media from the comfort of a temporary anchor chair. "I'm filling in for the vacationing Beatrice Brown today," he explained while his assistants directed camera shots and text feeds for his teleprompter. "It's a warm spring day here on Kodiak Island. This is more than a funeral and remembrances for friends and colleagues we lost just a few months ago. It's an inauguration of new facilities that are being built to replace what was destroyed and a confirmation of our purpose for being here."

* * *

What had been an afterthought many years ago, during some phase of launch complex expansion, was now important in ways that few could appreciate. National, state, and local dignitaries arrived at the recently updated cemetery, to be seated in climate controlled tents surrounded by their own security details. Members of the starport administration were given similar accommodations. Everyone had ample parking, with a good view of the manicured surroundings and turbulent sea.

Cameras and shotgun-style microphones were conveniently located on visible tripods in and around the area, giving excluded members of the infotainment universe a sense of participation through remote viewing options. Anyone who didn't want to be seen or heard could avoid these zones of coverage at their discretion. Global subscription rates skyrocketed when famous and well-known personalities began to eulogize James Cook and those who had died with him when the company's corporate headquarters was destroyed by saboteurs.

Politicians, astronauts, sports figures, and movie stars each took their turns in front of 33 ceremonial coffins draped with American and Alaskan flags. Most of them shared a short, fond memory about Jim. A few were too choked up to say more than a heartfelt goodbye.

Administrator Frost sat in the large, highly publicized pavilion, directly behind the platform that supported the lectern and its array of wireless microphones. With a smart phone in one hand, she listened to starport activity reports when they came in through her earpiece. The pageantry of speeches and ceremonies alternated in a pattern that allowed news programs around the world to get in some of their normal commercial breaks. These events included remarks from representatives of the U.S. Army, Air Force, and Coast Guard, who presided over a mournful rendition of "Taps."

* * *

Raven went to the podium after the last celebrity wrapped up his eulogy, walking away in tears.

"We make the future we want to live in," she began slowly. "Those words have been said by Governor Wheeler and more than a few of my predecessors, to include Jim Cook. They are more than a statement of fact. This phrase expresses what we intend to do. It's why we are here, now. In spite of…this."

Voices chattered quietly from the earpiece clipped to her coat collar while she spoke, letting Raven know what was going on behind the scenes. She read the podium's outdoor digital clock through the dark lenses of trendy eyewear.

"Making that future means more than building and flying rockets or shuttles. We ought to think of ourselves as gatekeepers, here to make sure that doorway to space remains open and unlocked for the next generation of pilots, explorers, and engineers. More than a corporate motto, it ought to be our calling."

Heads and cameras turned when the ground briefly shook. A silver needle on a swirling column of smoke and fire ascended noisily into the sky. Raven touched her naked wrist, knowing that her stainless steel trophy watch was attached to the payload that spectators on the ground and around the world were witnessing the launch of. "Amazing, isn't it? That's going up to work on the mess." She paused clumsily as the onlookers cheered. "We'll make room for new satellites in low orbit within two years."

Air traffic controllers at the starport reacted to Raven's verbal cue, granting clearance for six of Norman Ahgupuk's modified F-15s to slowly fly over the cemetery in a traditional 'missing man' formation at a low altitude. They passed overhead and out to sea in a thunderous roar that lasted 50 seconds.

"There is nothing about this or any other crisis we can't overcome—if we want to," she maintained, raising her voice. "Countries, corporations, or humanity—we've all got our problems! Food, water, money. We need them, to one extent or another. As the current administrator of this starport, it will be my honor and my responsibility to play any role, no matter how small, in making that better world for everyone, no matter who you are or where you live!"

EPILOGUE

Audiovisual records from the period corroborate wartime activities of key starport personnel as they occurred. Major happenings were observed by mainstream media sources and various government agencies of their day, as represented in this dramatic recreation.

Questions remain about the chronology of events on the ground at the Kodiak Starport during the aerospace attack. Evidence, in the form of department reports and after action case studies, has been missing from company archives for quite some time. Official documents granting immunity from federal prosecution for senior starport figures are a matter of public record. The motives and responsibilities of the individuals named continue to be examined by historians.

Equipment failures and contractor malfeasance are given as reasons for loss of company records. Federal officials report similar gaps for similar reasons, leading many to wonder if a cover-up was arranged. A series of privately funded investigations have all reached differing conclusions, which hasn't satisfied contemporary readers.

Efforts made to save the facility from destruction during that conflict are still debated at length in university classrooms and executive training seminars when issues of corporate responsibility are examined. The tenure of Jim Cook is regarded as the end of an era in which starport administrators acted with total, unrestricted authority.

The technologies developed in such places may be just what we need to save our dying world or relocate to a new planet that has enough resources to give us a second chance. Is that potential for advancement and expansion so important to our long-term future as a species that it warrants a special arrangement with our terrestrial governments?

About the Author

Justin Oldham is a legally blind writer who lives in Anchorage, Alaska. He holds bachelor's degrees in political science and history. Other works of fiction include *Bibix*, *Tales from the Kodiak Starport*, and *Crisis at the Kodiak Starport*. His nonfiction works include *Being Legally Blind: Observations for Parents of Visually Impaired Children*, *Your Ocular Prosthetic*, and *Living with Low Vision*.

Justin has always been fascinated by the pioneers of aviation and aerospace who took mankind from the ground into the stars. Their examples inspired him to write about a future in which space travel is more consequential to the human experience.

A long-time Alaskan resident, Justin's many interests include collecting books related to the Cold War and 20th century science fiction. Reading, writing, playing strategy games, and home improvement projects keep him busy.

For more information about the author, visit his website at http://www.justinoldham.com. For more about Justin's books, visit our website at http://www.shadowfusionbooks.com.

CPSIA information can be obtained
at www.ICGtesting.com
Printed in the USA
LVHW081053290122
709439LV00028B/150

9 781935 964704